Alice J. Harris-Wood is the founder of The Fisher House, a group home for seniors. She wanted a place they could call home which provided all services at an affordable price. As a high school teacher, local civic leader, and church music director, she excelled. She is well known in her town and surrounding areas for many years of dedicated service. Her dedication and success came from having a strong family foundation.

In loving memory of my uncle, Harvey Harris, who was a very kind and loving man, a man who knew the past and was not afraid to share the family history.

Alice J. Harris-Wood

CRIMINAL DEFENSE

AUSTIN MACAULEY PUBLISHERS™

LONDON · CAMBRIDGE · NEW YORK · SHARJAH

Ordering Information:
Quantity sales: special discounts are available on quantity purchases by corporations, associations, and others. For details, contact the publisher at the address below.

Publisher's Cataloging-in-Publication data
Harris-Wood, Alice J.
Criminal Defense

ISBN 9781643781525 (Paperback)
ISBN 9781643781532 (Hardback)
ISBN 9781645367086 (ePub e-book)

The main category of the book — FICTION / Crime

Library of Congress Control Number: 2019911577

www.austinmacauley.com/us

First Published (2019)
Austin Macauley Publishers LLC
40 Wall Street, 28th Floor
New York, NY 10005
USA

mail-usa@austinmacauley.com
+1 (646) 5125767

Introduction

Criminals are among us all but Lola was a criminal by way of genetic defect. She was born to be a criminal and only her family history would set her free from going to jail for a long time or maybe for life.

Lola was desperate and she needed to reveal the crimes of her forefathers in order to avoid going to jail. This is a story about love, revenge, murder, racketeering, prostitution, and many other crimes that were committed by the Harrison family dating back to the early 1900s.

Each generation was of career criminals who loved that lifestyle. Lola never tried to be anything but a criminal until she found herself sitting in a dark, smelly jail cell. The past had caught up with her. She was the first of the entire family of criminals to land in a jail holding cell.

The Harrison family, throughout the years, had to overcome many challenges in order to survive. Each generation changed the way they made money, handled criminal activities, and passed the wealth down to the next generation. Along with wealth, they passed the criminal genes. Each generation loved that life.

As the family history was passed down to the next generations and as the family members fell in love and got married, the color of the family changed. This family never showed any signs of being prejudiced and in fact did not even think about color. It was only a problem when outsiders became aware that this was an interracial family made up of black and white family members.

The Harrison family endured many ups and downs but always landed on their feet. At the end, the family came to Lola's defense, starting with the forefathers. This story is all about a family of criminals and how they came together to save Lola.

Alice J. Harris Wood is the youngest of thirteen children whose parents were from Littleton, N.C. Her father, mother, uncles, and aunts did whatever it took to survive. If it meant being a criminal, that is how they lived. Many of the fictional characters and events came from actual family criminal behaviors. The Harrison family members were true survivors. None of them ever went to jail, not even Lola.

The Beginning Generation of Criminals

'This is a dark place, the voices are loud, and it is cold and dirty. How did I allow myself to become part of this? Does anyone care? I hope no one touches me. If they do, I will scream, but will anyone hear? Deep down inside of me, I know my life has been wrong, but am I responsible or was it in my genes?' Lola's conversation with herself caused tears to flow down her pretty, cream-colored, small, smooth face. Her hair was without any shape but it was still pretty, even though it needed a good shampooing.

Lola sat quietly in the corner on the floor, hoping that the love of her life would come and rescue her. She waited and waited and no one came. 'Does anyone care?' she said to herself. She could hear different names being called, but not hers. Lola knew that in order to survive, she had to save herself. At that moment, she relaxed and accepted the fact that this was the holding cell for jail. Her next move would be leaving to go up to the big house (jail).

'I must understand my past in order to defend my future,' thought Lola. 'Who can I turn to, who knows the past? How did I become a gangster, a madam, and a drug kingpin all in one body and end up in jail maybe for life? Oh, I know the past because of what my grandparents left behind.'

Lola looked up from her small space in the cell and there was a tall, good-looking young man who looked like he just stepped out of a magazine. His body was that of an athlete and she could smell his cologne that was lightly covering his body. His light golden skin and bedroom eyes made him a very handsome man. As he was kneeling down towards her, Lola thought, 'Is he the one?'

'He is a black man, but I believe he is the right man for me,' thought Lola.

"Are you Miss Lola?" asked the man softly.

"Yes," replied Lola, "and are you my prince who has come to rescue me?"

"Rescue, I don't know but defend you, yes. You are accused of racketeering, drugs selling, prostitution, and illegal liquor sales etc."

With his head low, Ted spoke in a very low voice so that others could not hear him. "This is my first case with such heavy charges. I am a specialist in traffic violations and was forced to handle this case for my boss. My boss is a good friend of your Uncle Nick and he was asked to get you out of this mess at any cost."

"Then congratulations, you are a winner on your first criminal case. I got it all figured out. Just listen to my story and follow my lead. I come from good stock. Redd's children did not produce any dummies. You go and come back with a tape recorder and I will tell my story and the court will be understanding."

"I have a tape recorder with me," said Ted. "Start from the beginning."

"Redd was my grandfather. He was an Irishman from Harrisonville, N.C."

Sitting in this dark corner, not wanting anyone to touch her, and smelling bad odors brought back memories of her family's past which created a hot fire in her chest that only the truth could put out. The bootlegging, speakeasies, the ladies of the night, and the reputation of not giving a damn was all turning around in her head.

She took a deep breath and decided if she could explain her ancestry to this man and the court, then an angel from heaven would descend upon her and raise her up from this hellhole and lead her on to live a righteous life. This was all that she had that she could hold on to.

"I believe it all started around early 1900s when my grandfather was a teenager. They called him Redd because he had red skin with dark, curly black hair. He was Irish. My father would say, 'My father was the godfather of the South and he was a genius and I loved him. He was my role model. When I grow up, I want to be just like him.'

"My father got his wish because he was a chip off the old block. He was the godfather of the South, South Harrisonville County.

"'Do not drop any of that corn or the husk because we need it all. I have two types of moonshine to make, one for the blacks and one for the whites. This farm is a moneymaker, not a money-loser. I pay good wages for a good day's work. If you cannot work, you will be replaced now and not tomorrow. Therefore, keep pushing and keep working,' said Redd as he looked over his workers.

"'Redd, the moonshine orders are coming in faster than we can make the liquor,' said his foreman.

"'Keep the orders coming, we can build more stills. Call Harry and tell him to get over here, now. He needs to set up three more stills.'

"According to my father, Redd was a fair man who migrated here from the old country and believed in a day's work for a day's pay. If you could not do the work, then you were out of here. Deep in the swamp, the stills were laid out and organized like tombstones in a graveyard. One side produced the mild stuff that was made from corn and the other side produced the hellfire that was said to put hair on your chest; it was made from the cornhusk.

"Redd said to his operator, 'I do not care if the blacks buy the hellfire; if they got the money, then we got the time to sell. Money is money. I don't give a damn where it comes from. White power, black power, but green power is the only power that counts to me.'

"As the sun went down, many of the white men from the area would visit 'Redd's Do Drop Inn' and chill out from a long hard day's work. 'Welcome, have a good time but do not start anything or there will be two hits. I will hit you and you will hit the floor,' said Redd. Redd was a big man, about 6'10" and smart. He practiced what he preached.

"Do Drop Inn was a place for men only, but one day Redd was informed that Jumbo, a competitor, started having a white woman in his place serving men their drinks. This did not sit well with Redd, so he decided to have a black woman serving drinks and cooking food. This brought his regulars back but the competitor did not stop trying to steal Redd's customers. Therefore, Redd decided to put an end to all of this nonsense.

"Redd said to his operator, 'Get me my shotgun, my black horse, and five guys. This bastard is dead meat tonight. I am sick of this shit. I have given him many opportunities to leave my business alone and now it is time to take action. I will buy him out or put him out.'

"It was raining hard but Redd did not care. He was on a mission to put this sucker out of business tonight. The six of them rode for over an hour to Jumbo's spot. Redd went in with his back-up behind him and his shotgun ready to fire. He walked right over to Jumbo and said in a soft voice, 'Jumbo, you have two options. You can leave and give your place to me or go six feet under. Which one you choose makes no difference to me. This place belongs to me tonight.'

"Jumbo knew of Redd's reputation and looked him dead in the eye, then lowered his head, and without looking up walked out. Redd yelled out, 'Let the good times roll! Fiddler, play some music, and you women push the tables back and grab a man, and let's dance. The moonshine is on me tonight.'

"Redd, on his way home with his men, was ambushed by Jumbo and his gang. Redd's horse was shot from under him and he was able to hide in the woods. The other men were all slaughtered. Redd waited until the hunt for him was over and headed home. As the sun was coming up, he stumbled into the kitchen and passed out on the floor.

"When he woke up, he said, 'With God as my witness, my family and I will never be defeated again by any man. We might be down but we will never be out.' He said to Rita, who was his wife, 'I want a breakfast fit for a king. For as of this day, I am the king. The Moonshine King, the only go-to guy. Without me, no things will move or happen.' Rita quickly got his breakfast together and called their two sons to come and eat.

"Nate and Nick, who were twins, came to the table as if it was time for a new lesson in life. They were right; it was a lesson on life that would be their family code that was to be adhered to at any cost.

"'Okay,' said Redd, 'this is the first day of us building an empire and to let our customers and clients know that we are open for business and we are the business.'

"Redd took a deep breath and looked around, nodding his head, and after a few minutes, yelled, 'I will not be undersold! I will do to others before they do to me! I will never be defeated. (I might be out but not down.) I will do whatever it takes to keep my family safe and to feed them. I will kill to keep the family name intact for future generations. I will never be scared to die.'

"'Boys, finish your meal, for we have some business to take care of today,' said Redd.

"'What kind of business, Pop?' asked Nick, looking concerned. (He was the older of the two boys by one minute.)

"'All I am going to tell you at this point is that you will not be disappointed.'

"Redd, Nick, and Nate saddled up their horses and off they went, heading towards Jumbo's bar. Redd had in his saddle bags everything he needed to accomplish his mission. The boys still did not know the mission but it was understood that someone was not going to be happy in a few hours.

"The bar was closed because it did not open until late afternoon. Redd knew this and it was part of his plan. He did not want anyone but Jumbo to get hurt. He just wanted to eliminate Jumbo as a competitor and make him pay for the killing of his six men. His plan was a two-part plan. First burn down the bar and then find Jumbo and kill him for killing his men.

"When they got to the bar, Redd handed Nick and Nate several bottles of kerosene with a flaming rag hanging from the top. 'Throw the bottles, boys. Throw it now!' Redd yelled.

They threw the bottles and the wood building went up in flames.

Jumbo was inside and came running out, shouting, 'I will kill you, Irish trash.'

"This really set Redd off. 'I will make sure that you will not have to see this trash ever again. You poor white scumbag,' said Redd (with a look on his face that would have scared God). He rode right up to Jumbo and put his shotgun up against his head and pulled the trigger. Redd said in a voice that sounded like a priest, 'One more sinner going straight to hell.'

"Before the dust had settled over this situation, Redd took the bodies of his six men to the sheriff's office and told what had happened earlier.

"'I will take care of everything; you know you are my best friend. I will always have your back. You have taken care of this town and all that comes in contact with you. We, here in Harrisonville, respected your father and that is why this town is named after your family. You are our largest employer. I am your partner and so is this town,' said the sheriff.

"Redd's mind was always turning, trying to come up with new ways to make money and keep control in his hands. That day he was back, talking and encouraging his workers to work harder and longer or someone else could replace them. 'Work harder, work longer, or you will be replaced!' Redd yelled.

"Rita called the family together for dinner. Redd had dreamed about his plans for building an empire of business enterprises, some legal and some illegal. The legal ones he would use to shelter the illegal businesses. At dinner, he laid out his entire plan for expansion.

"As Redd started speaking, Nick and Nate glanced back and forth toward each other. They knew that his plans were well thought-out and that they were to play a major part.

"'Okay, boys,' said Redd, 'this is the plan. I will lay the whole organization out along with the system. My first cousin who lives in upstate PA has suddenly died. He was an only child and his parents died about ten years ago. He had bird seeds for a brain. He owned about one hundred and seventy-five acres of farm, forest, and swampland. Can you believe all that to an idiot who was just a waste of meat?'

"Nick asked, 'How did he die? Why didn't we know about this cousin?'

"'Well boys, the reason you did not know about him was that he was not worth talking about. The farm was being run by a friend who was stealing everything from him. So I stopped that. I visited my cousin last summer for a few days and had him do two things. I knew what needed to be done, so I did it. He made a will leaving everything to his beloved first cousin who grew up with him like a brother. You know that was a lie. Next, I became his power of attorney.'

"'Well, Pop,' the boys said at the same time, 'does this story have an interesting ending?'

"'Yes, because I caused it to have a great ending. Later I found out that he had a $100,000.00 paid up whole life insurance policy which was purchased by his parents when he was a baby. I made myself the sole beneficiary. It was a pity that his breaks on his truck failed and he ran into a tree and was thrown out of the truck and the truck ran over him and he was killed instantly,' said Redd.

"'Oh my,' said Nick.

"'Unbelievable,' said Nate.

"Little did they know that Redd had his cousin killed.

"'The police called and told me that he died. My cousin is in heaven. He was a dun but he never hurt anyone,' said Redd as he closed his eyes and said a short prayer.

"Redd spoke like a priest, 'This man is going straight to heaven and that is a fact.'

"'Now that we have more land and more money, we can start our building of the empire that will be passed down to other generations. To start with, I want to send Nate to Georgia to work the land and the area,' Pop spoke like a general in the army. 'You will find a woman and make her your wife. Make sure that you do love her and she is pretty. Have lots of children. By doing this, everyone will see you as a family man with many business ties. Your main crop will be corn. In the swamp, you will set up your stills. You will open up several bars that are legal and sell our moonshine. I will handle the distribution of moonshine to other parts of Georgia. You will find the drivers and I will guarantee the delivery. If trouble finds you, take care of it, but inform me before you kill anyone.

"'In your bars, hire fast women and offer good hometown cooking and music and keep the music going with dancing. It should be non-stop all night until the sun comes up. Have several guards at the door to throw out rough people. If the peace officers come, pay them off, and give them a bottle of our best moonshine,' said Redd as he started to stand up.

"'Keep an eye on the money! Have your wife be in charge of finances. Make an example out of someone who you know is stealing from you. This can be done in several ways. One is to cut off their hand or just kill them. Whatever happens, you have to maintain your laws and your order.

"'If it appears that you are having a problem with the peace officers, send your wife over to charm them and to settle the problem,' Redd said with a deep conviction that this was the right course to take."

Lola stopped talking and was having a hard time keeping the family ancestry history going. Lola said, remembering what her father would say about her mother, "What his Georgia Peach wanted, she got." She was thinking about her father's saying as she surveyed this gorgeous creature. Ted was great-looking with smooth, light brown skin and pretty, brown, bedroom eyes. The aroma coming from his clothes was sending her straight to the bedroom. His eyes reminded her of her brother.

"Oh my," said Lola in a low, soft voice.

"What was that you said, Miss Lola?" Ted asked, looking totally involved.

"I was thinking about something my father would say about my mother," said Lola.

"Lola, let's continue with your defense because what you have given me so far will not get you a reduced sentence or get you off altogether," replied Ted.

"It was told to me that Redd had even bigger and better plans for Nick," said Lola.

"Redd turned to Nick, who was the younger twin, and said, 'You are a lot like me. I know it is in the genes. You think things through, you take action, and you will deliver. In this line of work, having all those attributes will make for an important man in this competitive field of business. Therefore, I have laid the ground work for you but all the small details of how to accomplish your mission will be up to you.' Redd sounded like the good father giving his son some advice on how to make an honest living. "'I have some very important friends in Philadelphia and New York. I have sent word that you will be there by the end of the month. They will provide you with two rows of homes in South Philly. You will take the money that I will give you and renovate the buildings by tearing down the joining walls. This will allow for a larger home. The home will have two basements, eight bedrooms, two kitchens, two bathrooms, one large living room, and one large dining room.' Redd spoke as if he had a list written in his brain.

"'You will put bars up at all the windows; this will keep the peace officers out until you can close down your activities,' said Redd.

"'I guess you want me to decide what activities will be going on at my home,' said Nick.

"'Yes and no,' replied Redd.

"'My friends will teach you the business. Do not, under any circumstances, get married or fall in love. That will truly be your downfall. A woman in this business is a liability that will be hard to overcome. As you get further into the business, you will understand.' Redd spoke these words like a man who had been there and done that.

"Rita was a woman that he married to help raise his two boys. But he did not love her like a lover, only as a partner raising children, cleaning, and cooking. She did love him and was willing to settle for that small part of him.

"Redd's first wife was named Nina. She was slightly tall, thin, with silky smooth creamy skin, and long, dark brown thick hair. No matter where she went, all heads would turn. She was beautiful from head to toe. She knew she was blessed with many of the benefits of beauty that most people could only dream about.

"Nina was very smart and at an early age decided what road she would travel in life. Her road consisted of having men adore her for money. She learned the business from an older girl, who was about twenty-two years old, who saw potential in Nina. She took one look at her and became Nina's good friend. Her name was Candee and she had total control over her new young friend Nina who was sixteen years old.

"'I want more than anything to use my gifts that God has given me to make men happy and at the same time become very wealthy,' Nina spoke these words to Candee as she was laying out Nina's future.

"'To begin with,' said Candee, 'all types of men are going to try to claim you. Do not let that happen. If you do, your chosen career will be over.

"'You must be sure this is what you want,' said Candee in a very directing voice. 'Never have sex with any customers. That is never acceptable in the business that we are going to introduce to this county.'

"'How do I start?' asked Nina.

"'Tell your parents that you have a job in the next county,' said Candee.

"'I do not have any parents or any relatives but have always wished for a family of my own one day,' revealed Nina.

"'Well, you can start by calling me Candee. How's that?' said Candee as she smiled.

"'I have foster parents who will be happy to know that I am leaving. They were friends of my parents and took me in and gave me a place to live,' said Nina as she looked hopeful about her future.

"'I have dreamed of starting this business. I have most of the details worked out. Money will not be an issue because I have a boyfriend that just loves me. In fact, he wants to marry me but I am scared,' said Candee.

"'My friend's name is Buddy. He is a good-looking guy. He has never been married; I would be the first. The first Mrs. Buddy and the wife of a true criminal sounds like a good future. Buddy is involved in many activities but I act as though I do not know. I did some research on him and found out he is the boss in Harrisonville County. He is worth millions,' said Candee, who spoke like an authority figure.

"'He once told me he had a business partner named Redd. They grew up together like brothers. Redd and Buddy have been friends since the age of sixteen. I have never seen this Redd character but from what Buddy told me, he is someone worth knowing,' implied Candee.

"'Well, I would like to meet someone nice one day, but for now I just want to get our business off the ground,' said Nina.

"'Okay, let's see. I will ask Buddy to give me one of his buildings for our saloon. We will open up late and stay open until daybreak. We will sell food that is cooked by the blacks in the area. They are the only ones in this county that can cook. Their cooking is so good that men will be asking us to sell them food to take home. Our clients will be men and women. We will also sell corn liquor supplied by Redd and his gang. The music will be played by the blacks because they know how to get it going. The singers can be white or black as long as they can sing and the customers can dance," said Candee.

"'I have a few ideas,' said Nina. 'In a totally different area of the building, maybe the basement, we can have a special place for men and women who want to get together to socialize. I can run that part of the business. I will charge the men by the hour for the room and pay the woman per client. This part of the business will be open twenty-four hours and every day of the week. Is there a name for this type of business, Candee?' asked Nina, looking very innocent.

"'Yes, a gentlemen's basement,' replied Candee in a joking way.

"'Great, that is what we will call my area of expertise. The Gentlemen's Basement,' said Nina.

"'I will call my business Candee's Palace,' said Candee in a sweet, low, sexy voice.

"'I will get in touch with Buddy and run our plans past him. I know he will like the idea and will also be extending the services that we plan to provide. He thinks big and goes big with everything,' said Candee.

"Buddy had several businesses. They included farming (produce and livestock), rental properties, rooming homes, speakeasies, moonshine/liquor-producing, gambling, banking, and insurance. Buddy grew up the hard way, fending for himself, because his father was killed while robbing a bank and his mother gave him away, after the death of his father, to a preacher and his wife who did not have any children. When Buddy got the chance, he stole the church offering and took off. He was on his way to anywhere except that town.

"He landed in Harrisonville and met Redd. Redd's genes for criminal activities matched up with Buddy's perfectly and they were friends instantly. Redd's experience from the old country made him the perfect partner in crime.

"Their empire all started with the introduction of making outstanding corn liquor that could be produced quickly without losing its quality. As times changed, they changed and they got involved in legal businesses that were profitable but at the same time concealed their true vocation. That is, professional gangsters."

Ted asked the jail attendant if he could have a private room to interview his client. As they were walking to the room, Ted walked slightly behind Nina. He started looking at her feet. He could see her toes in the flip flops that she was wearing and noticed that her feet were well kept. Her toes were manicured with a bright red polish that matched her lips and accented the shape and beauty of her feet.

As his eyes rolled upwards, her legs were perfect in shape and size. The short skirt she was wearing could only be worn by her. Anyone else would have destroyed the design. Ted thought to himself, 'There must be a God that made such a beautiful creature.'

Lola's waist was just the right size to hold tight as a lover would in order to make love with her. Her breast was small but sweet to look at. She was wearing a spaghetti-strapped top with a low-cut front.

Ted tried to stop himself from looking at Lola but was unable to control his eyes. His eyes wandered up to her neck and that is when he stopped walking behind her and rushed up to open the door.

"After you, lovely lady," Ted spoke like a gentleman.

"Lola, your family history is getting very interesting and I want to hear more," said Ted.

"Okay, there is plenty more to tell. This family of mine never gave me a chance in life to be an honest working person. It is really not their fault, for it is all about the genes," said Lola as she started sitting in the cushioned chair.

"Candee sent word to Buddy that she wanted to see him and it was all about business. Buddy knew that Redd was his best friend and partner and that all business must be discussed amongst the three of them.

"'I love Candee, Redd. Hopefully one day she will marry me. She has everything a man like me needs, but she changes the subject every time I come close to talking about future plans with her,' said Buddy with a sad look on his face.

"'Well, my friend, I will never fall in love. I love the single life. Having a different woman every night and loving it. Marriage will never work for me. I do not want someone asking me questions, like where are you going, when will you be back, and that suit does not look good on you. To hell with married life! I love this life and it cannot get any better than this. Trust me, friend, we are better off single,' Redd spoke like a true friend.

"Buddy had a key to Candee's home. He opened the door and Redd and Buddy just walked right in. Walking in without being announced made Buddy feel like a husband. This gave him a pleasant feeling about his relationship with Candee.

The two girls were sitting on the sofa having a drink when the men entered. 'This is my cousin, Nina. She will be staying with me until she gets her own place, okay boys?' said Candee in a low, sexy voice.

"The two men looked like schoolboys that just saw their first look at a woman's body. Their feet were frozen to the floor. No words were able to be formed because their jaws were shut tight and locked. Candee kept yelling Buddy's name but he did not respond. Finally, Nina got up and went towards Redd and kissed him on his lips. At that point, he came back and was astonished and shocked.

"Everything Redd had said about not falling in love was gone. He was in love at the sight of this beautiful woman. 'You are gorgeous. You are gorgeous. You are gorgeous,' said Redd, with no control of his words.

"'Redd, Redd, Redd, snap out of it. Pull yourself together,' said Candee.

"'Guys, come and sit down and have a strong drink,' said Candee in strong, commanding voice.

"'To start with, this is my cousin and she is a beauty. She is young but willing to learn the business,' said Candee.

"After taking a few slips of his drinks, Buddy said, 'What do you mean by learning the business?'

"'I have been with you for many years. Long before you became rich with influence. Your banking operation, insurance business, and the gambling enterprises have survived because of the long hours and hard work that I have devoted to the business. It is my time to open up a new business of my own with my cousin. I have many of the details worked out. I will start small and expand in a few years,' said Candee in a demanding voice.

"'So, tell me what you want, my love,' said Buddy.

"'To begin with, you can see that Nina is beautiful. With her beauty and my business knowledge, we can get it right the first time. What is needed is a nice-looking, big building in town. We want it to be accessible to customers who are walking or riding. I'd like to open a saloon. It will be called 'Candee's Palace.' I will serve alcohol, food, music, and dancing. It will be like a New York City Club but located in Harrisonville. It will be glamorous with pretty girls serving drinks and food. The music will be live with a band and singers. The customers can dance or sit and enjoy the music,' said Candee, looking very calculating.

"'In the basement, Nina will be dressed like a porcelain doll baby. Part of the basement will be for men who want to socialize with a beautiful woman like Nina. She will run that business. Located in the basement will be another business that will help to expand your current business like poker games. Even though the basement is illegal, there should not be much of a problem because of your influence with top-elected officials and the local law enforcement. Many of them will also be patrons of the 'Gentlemen's Basement,' said Candee.

"'If we have room, there can also be a number writing business for your bookies,' said Candee, looking business-like. As you can see, I have been thinking about this for a long time and Nina came into my life and gave me hope, excitement, and energy to take on such a big project,' Candee spoke like a professional businesswoman.

"'Yes, it is obvious that this is what you want. It is also what I want for you. We can work out the details later but there is one thing I would want from you. Let's go into the other room. This is between you and me,' said Buddy.

"Candee did not know what to expect, so she just followed Buddy into the other room without any resistance.

"Redd looked at Nina and walked right up to her without blinking his eyes. 'I do not believe I am saying this but you will be my wife? I cannot help myself but no other woman has ever turned me on like you. I just met you for the first time. It is also the first time I met your cousin. Buddy talks about her all the time. I think if she asked him to go straight and be honest, he would do just that. I could never understand his love for this woman but now I understand,' said Redd with a very sober face.

"Nina looked at Redd and felt the same way, love at first sight. 'I do not want a short romance before I tie the knot,' thought Nina. 'Therefore, I will have him wine and dine me for a while or until I am twenty-one,' she thought as she analyzed the situation.

"Redd's beautiful, curly black hair and red face made him look outstanding. He was dressed splendidly from neck to his feet. 'He is a tall, slender man with a good speaking voice,' thought Nina. 'He could have been anything in this world if he wanted it. But Redd chose to be a gangster.' She was thinking to herself as she looked him up and down in a girlish demeanor.

"'Nina, do you think I can meet your family soon?' asked Redd.

26

"'Ho, you do move quickly. Well, you see, Redd, Candee is all I have and you met her tonight,' said Nina. 'Therefore, we can skip the family thing and go to dinner soon, okay?' said Nina.

"'That sounds like a lady who knows what she wants and how to get it,' thought Redd.

"'We will go to the finest place to dine in this state. That is my golf club's country club,' said Redd with great joy.

"'What should I wear to the club, Redd? You know I am just a small-town country girl,' said Nina, looking naïve.

"'You will look good in anything but if it will make you happy, then we will go shopping for all new clothes for an all new you. I will be the envy of every man in this county. One day, I will be pleased to announce that you are my fiancée,' said Redd.

"Voices were coming from the other room that sounded happy. At this point, Buddy and Candee entered the room. 'Hey guys, we have some good news to tell you,' said Buddy. 'My lovely lady has finally agreed to marry me. To make sure she does not change her mind, we are getting married in two months,' said Buddy, speaking like the happiest man in the world.

"Redd went home and Buddy stayed with Candee that night. Buddy could not get Candee out of his mind, for he had tunnel vision. All he could see and think about was Candee.

"The next day, Buddy got busy making plans for the wedding with Candee. First he sent for all his staff. The business was really one business, that business of making money from any source. His staff was his lawyer, his accountant, and Candee his manager.

"'Candee and I are going to get married in two months. I want to invite all the state and local politicians, law enforcement captains that are on our payroll, plus local residents and friends. Whatever number it comes to is okay with us. We want this to be the wedding of the century. Do you understand?' implied Buddy.

"Next on Buddy's list was Candee's new business. 'Candee has come up with a great idea, which is to start a club called Candee's Palace. We need a location that is easy to get to, in which anyone who wants to come can walk or ride. I have a building that I won in a poker game just outside of town. It is the old Miller mansion. It is located on a hill with plenty of space and land for parking and other activities for our patrons. Candee, maybe it should be called Miller Hill!' shouted Buddy.

"Smiling and looking quite pleased, Candee said, 'Sounds good to me. Let's go with it.'

"'Buddy, can we have the wedding at the country club?" asked Candee.

"'This is why I love you; we think alike. That is just what I was going to suggest to you,' said Buddy.

"Buddy was a good manager. The whole town was involved in getting Miller Hill ready for its grand opening for New Year's Eve and at the same time preparing the guest list, the food, and all the other things that go into planning a wedding. This was a great time for Harrisonville. There was plenty of excitement in the air. People were buzzing around, happy with the feeling of nothing but joy that was on its way."

"Did they get married, Buddy and Candee?" asked Ted.

"Yes, and it was everything that Candee could have dreamed," replied Lola.

"Buddy and Redd were part owners of the club with fifty-five percent. Redd believed that it would not be good for business if the membership knew they were owners," said Lola.

"The bank, as it was called, lent money to clients that could not borrow money from a government-regulated bank. Their clients came from all over the county. Some were well-educated who needed money for a start-up business. On the other hand, some just needed it to make it to the next payday. Whatever the situation was, the bank would lend the money with a high interest rate. In some cases, it was as high as sixty percent. Sixty percent if they did not have any assets to use as collateral," said Lola.

"A payment with interest had to be made every week or Candee would send her collector to get the payment. The uncollected interest was added to the principal and when the balance was over a certain amount, an insurance policy would be taken out on the client, with Candee as the beneficiary," Lola looked concerned as she spoke.

"Did they ever collect on the insurance policies?" asked Ted.

"Sure, all the time," said Lola.

"This was a group of people that you did not want to owe anything," said Lola.

"If you did, you either paid up or died," said Lola with certainty.

"The swampland on Redd's farm was the graveyard for poor souls who could not pay. After about a year of being missing, Candee would stake a claim and the adjustor who was on their payroll would submit the claim to the insurance company and Candee would get paid," confessed Lola.

"Getting back to the country club's ownership and how the two friends became partners, Redd was very good at poker and the owner of the club was a regular at his weekend poker games. In order to play in these games, you had to buy in with at least two thousand dollars. The owner lost a lot of money playing poker and always thought he could win his money back. Without realizing it, he was borrowing from the bank. Because he wanted large sums, his country club had to be put up as collateral. He was making his payments on time but the business slowed down and he had a problem with his cash flow. He started missing payments and that was not a good thing to do.

"So Candee told the boys, 'We need to become his partners. Let him be the front man but we will control the money and business.' At first, the owner did not like the idea but he realized it was not worth dying for his country club. And that is just what would happen. He would have been lying in the swamp of poor souls," said Lola.

"The old plantation on the hill was the center of attention for Harrisonville. Unemployment in this town was very low. The only people that were not working were little kids and real old people. The plantation's new name was Miller Hill. It needed a lot of work but Buddy and Redd did not care, for it was for their two lovely women.

"Miller Hill was not always a happy place. It was almost destroyed by the union soldiers during the war but was purchased later by a plantation owner in the area. He worked in the farm but after the slaves were freed, he could not afford to keep them or the plantation. He had two children and a wife who he loved. As he sat next to his fireplace with very little to eat but drinking whisky and getting more and more depressed, he took his shotgun and killed his whole family while they were sleeping in their beds and then killed himself too. He left a note stating that he could not bear the fact that they were going to be put out on the street by the bank because the mortgage was a year behind," said Lola in a low and sober voice.

"After many, many years of sitting abandoned, the boys purchased it from the bank for almost nothing. The bank just wanted to get rid of it," said Lola.

"The boys felt good and alive again. They were both in love and nothing could stop them now," said Lola.

"Redd said, 'Before we do anything, let's set up a production plan and management plan so that we will be the greatest place in the state to eat, drink, gamble, and have fun with the ladies.'

"'Okay,' said Buddy. 'Candee, you and Nina work with our accountant to develop a plan for money and how it will be implemented.'

"'Yes, we will, my love,' said Candee. 'First I need to call a meeting with our friends in high places to let them know and understand that we need their cooperation and help to make Miller Hill a complete success. I will make it perfectly clear that they will be well compensated for their services,' said Candee.

"Candee was all business and most of the time had a pleasant, pretty smile on her face. But it was also known by all who knew her that her nickname was the smiling assassin. She would smile and be nice and then order you to be killed without you even knowing what she was going to do.

"She was also loved by all that met her. She was a very gracious lady. Only a handful of her closest associates knew the true Candee and that is how she wanted it and lived," said Lola.

"The plans for Miller Hill called for a large, big porch with two large white columns, one on each side of the door as you entered the front door. The windows in the front would start at the top of the first floor and ended a few inches from the floor. The plans called for two huge windows on each side.

"As you entered the front, there was to be a massive foyer with a gold-and-glass chandelier. The chandelier was to be imported from France. Candee wanted everything to remind the guest that this was a palace and it was a special place to be happy and have fun.

"'Miller Hill would be rocking and rolling every day of the week. It would have something for everyone. The ladies would enjoy the shows and dancing along with great food. If they had never been to Philadelphia or New York City, this would be a good substitute. The drinks would be served in fancy glasses and the waiters would be men with good service skills. Once inside, whatever you wanted, Miller Hill provided. No request would be too small or too big,' said Candee as she got excited by her own words.

"'Okay team,' said Candee, 'I want you to remember: customers come first. They are the reason for our business and not the cause of it,' said Candee as she smiled with total delight.

"'This is the plan. As you enter the foyer, you will be able to look up and see areas that gentlemen can take their wives or girlfriends or just a group of friends to, for dinner and drinks. As your eyes descend down, you will see a beautiful stage. In front of the stage at night would be a massive dance floor. Next will be small tables for two to four people to eat, drink, and be happy. Being happy is the name of the game. Happy people spend a lot of money. Do you understand, team?' said Candee.

"'I want everyone to leave, except Frank, who is the accountant and financial manager. Frank,' said Candee. 'Besides the night club, there will be other enterprises. The basement is the total length of this mansion. Therefore, Buddy,

Redd, and I want it utilized to the fullest. In order to do that, we are moving the bank, poker room, and bookie operation into the basement. There will also be an area of rooms for men who want the company of a beautiful lady. Frank, I want you to work with Nina to help set up the basement. It will be called the Gentlemen's Basement. It will look as elegant as the upper level or better for our customers,' said Candee.

"'A false wall will be designed to hide the basement door, just in case some of those religious nuts try to expose us. This area will be for existing customers who do not want anyone to know that they are patronizing the basement. It will have a bar and a dining area. Nina will run the Gentlemen's Basement and I will run Miller Hill. How does that sound, Frank?' said Candee.

"'When will we be up and running?' asked Frank.

"'Buddy wants it to be ready for business on New Year's Eve,' said Candee. 'Therefore we have four months to get everything in shape. How's that sound?' said Candee.

"'I believe it can be done, my lady,' replied Frank.

"Frank would do anything for Candee, for he also loved her but was never able to express it because he knew Buddy would have killed him," said Lola quietly as if Buddy might hear her.

"All the plans had been set in motion and everything was on schedule, for Miller Hill and religious groups had joined with other agitators to prohibit the sale of liquor by the federal government. The prohibition of liquor seemed sure to be passed and it was passed," said Lola.

"An emergency meeting was called for all the local officials and state lawmakers who were on the payroll to come together to work out a plan to keep the town from going belly-up. They met at Redd's place because it was far away from everything. The agitators did not know where Redd lived," said Lola.

"Did they solve the problem?" asked Ted.

"Well, solve the problem. That is a matter of how you see it," said Lola.

"This is how it is when down. Redd's family came from the old country, which was Ireland. His ancestors were the best bootleggers in that country. In fact, that is why they came to America; they were chased out of Ireland because of all their criminal activities. They were on the verge of being hung. They landed in Harrisonville and because of contagious deceases like whooping cough, his mother died soon after they got to Harrisonville," said Lola.

"Redd was smart and a quick learner. Therefore, he was able to set up stills and start selling moonshine. His buddies, the lawmakers and local law enforcers, decided they would ride it out with him until prohibition was overturned," said Lola.

"What about Miller Hill?" asked Ted.

"Miller Hill opened up on New Year's Eve as schedules with the local law officers as the security. Harrisonville felt that the rest of the country did not know them and they did not know the rest of the country. They believed that they had a right to work and make money for the town and feed their families," said Lola as she raised her voice.

"Miller Hill was rocking and rolling with Redd's moonshine every night. The band, piano, and singers were bringing customers from not just this county but from other states. The food was the best food throughout the South. The Gentlemen's Basement had a waiting list in order to get in. You waited upstairs until someone came and got you. One man left and another man came in," said Lola.

"The bank, the poker room, bookie parlor, and rooms for special visitors with lovely ladies were the hottest attractions throughout the South. Things were going very well and the money was rolling in. Redd was selling moonshine in almost every state on the east coast. Redd and Buddy were on top of the world. Nothing could stop them now," said Lola.

"This went on big for several years until prohibition was appealed. Then things got even better. Nina was now almost twenty-one years old and she was truly in love with Redd," said Lola. "So she decided it was time to be Redd's fiancée as he had predicted when she was only sixteen years old," said Lola, with tears in her eyes.

"'That night will be the night that I will have Redd to propose to me,' thought Nina. 'How will I do it? Should I get him drunk and just tell him in the morning after we made love that I said 'yes' to his marriage proposal? Oh, I know, I will put on the same dress that he first saw me in, with my bright red lipstick. Then when he comes through the door, I will walk up to him and kiss him on the forehead and he will understand that I am ready, ready to marry him,' Nina said to herself.

"Redd slowly opened the door and peeked in, for he was always surprised about something that Nina had done or was doing. Before he could get his head past the doorway, Nina grabbed and pulled him in. 'I am ready to get married, are you?'

"'Yes!' said Redd, 'let's go to Elkton, Maryland, tonight. That is where many of the famous celebrities go to get hooked up right away without any hassle or questions asked,' informed Redd.

"Nina replied, 'That sounds wonderful to me.'

"Nina threw a few things in her little red travel bag and off they went to get married. Nina left a note for Candee, stating that the time had come for her to be made an honest woman. 'Redd and I are on our way to Elkton, Maryland, to be married. I will see you in a few days, love Nina.'

"Maryland turned out to be a long way off; therefore, they stopped at a motel for the night. In that little red bag, Nina had a bottle of champagne with cheese and crackers. 'This is a night for making love and being loved,' thought Nina.

"That night, they made love like two teenagers who were stealing a small piece of time that could never be repeated like that night. The next day, they went to breakfast with just smiles of joy on their faces, not saying much to each other. They did not have to talk because they understood each other's deepest thoughts," said Lola.

"Walking down the streets of Elkton, Nina said, 'There, over there is where I want to get married. It looks like us,' said Nina.

"'You are right,' replied Redd. 'A small white building, with a white picket fence that looked like something out of a fairytale and that is how I feel, Nina,' said Redd.

"Nina read the sign which said: Wedding Chapel – All are welcome.

"As Nina and Redd walked in, they were greeted by a semi-fat lady with red, rosy cheeks. 'I love couples like you two, who are looking to be married for the rest of their lives,' said the lady. 'My name is Kate and I do it all. Are you ready to get married today?'

"Without hesitation, the two lovers said 'yes' at the same time.

Kate said, 'It will cost you $50.00 and if you want the full treatment, then it will be an extra $50.00.'

"Nina replied, 'What does the full treatment consist of?'

"'Well, love birds, my husband of forty years will play two songs, one before the service and one after the service. You can pick the songs from our book. It also includes fifty percent of a meal at the diner across the street. You will also receive a ticket for free parking in the lot where you are parked. How does that sound, love birds?' said Kate.

"'Well, give us the ticket for the parking and the music and you can have the meal ticket. I will be taking my wife to the airport for a honeymoon in the Bahamas. My friend is making the plans as we are speaking,' said Redd.

"In the motel, while Nina was sleeping, Redd placed a call to Buddy and told him that they were in to Elkton, Maryland, to get married in the morning. He asked him to make plans for them to fly to the Bahamas for their honeymoon of two weeks," said Lola.

Lola looked up at Ted and thought to herself, 'Wouldn't a two-week honeymoon with his hunk be just wonderful?'

'Lola and I could get a lot done with a two-week honeymoon,' said Ted to himself.

"How did the wedding turn out?" asked Ted.

"Just wonderful," replied Lola.

"Sure did, and they had no problem getting to the Bahamas," stated Lola.

"Redd had planned to go to the Bahamas to meet with some associates about bringing some ladies and some entertainers to Miller Hill. Therefore, he could combine business with pleasure," said Lola.

"In the Bahamas, business was conducted differently than in the States. Everyone wanted a piece of the action," said Lola.

"Nina understood Redd's desire to get some ladies and entertainers for Miller Hill. Therefore he wanted Nina to draw the associates in with him by using her charm," said Lola.

""Nina said, 'I have a plan. We will have a very outstanding dinner dance with all the most influential, important people in the area. Let's show them how rich we are and how we party. I will purchase a very expensive dress from one of their most exclusive stores in the area. When asked, I will tell the clerk that it is for a party for very exclusive group of people. The word will spread quickly and everyone who is someone will want to be invited.'

"'We will have the hall set up like Miller Hill. It will have a stage for the band and singers, a dance floor, and small tables for two to four people. All the waiters will be the best in business with good manners. Everything will be free. Anything that is requested will be provided,' said Redd.

"'My plan is to open up a Miller Hill in the Bahamas that Americans can take advantage of. It will be a totally legal operation. I have been tipped off by my friends in high places that the Feds are planning to audit our books. They are trying to get Buddy and me for tax evasion. Therefore, I want to hide my money here in the Bahamas and maybe we will have to leave the States and live here,' said Redd.

"'I will live anywhere with you, Redd,' replied Nina. 'You are my man for life.' Nina continued on saying that it sounded like a great plan to her and she loved the beaches and warm weather. 'The only thing that I have always wanted was a family. A house full of children. Is that okay with you, Redd, my love?" said Nina.

"Redd replied, 'I came from a family that was full of love. My father did whatever he could to provide a home and food for his wife and child. In the old country of Ireland, a man took care of his family and that is what my father did for us.'

"'Oh, Redd, you have made me very happy and I want to get started on our family as soon as possible,' replied Nina.

"Redd and Nina decided to extend their stay for an extra few weeks so that they could plan the greatest party the Bahamas had ever hosted. Nina was in charge of the total planning for this event. She wanted only the best of everything. Cost was not an issue with Nina. She considered it an investment.

"The menu was made up of only American foods. She sent for her chief in the States and he brought his entire crew of cooks and waiters. The chief was black and so was the crew. Next, she scheduled the performer to come on the day before the party so that they could rehearse with the local popular band.

"When she finished, the only thing that was needed was for her to develop a guest list. Therefore, she asked the head housekeeper in the hotel to help her with the list. The head housekeeper knew all the important people in all of the Bahamas and adjacent islands. Nina left that up to Tanya, the hotel's head housekeeper.

"Buddy's job was to find a fantastic building that could hold around five hundred people. Buddy was thinking about the future. The building that was going to be used for the party would be the new Miller Hill, but this new location would need a new name. Therefore, he wanted Nina's opinion on the name.

There were several buildings that he looked at but was not satisfied and he was starting to get depressed. Just at that moment, his guide Lyle said, 'I know what you want, a place that makes the guests feel good and so they will return often to have a good time.'

"'That's right, my friend,' replied Redd.

"Lyle was a very good-looking businessman who had a dream of his own but did not have the money to make his dream come true. But with Redd as his backer, it would be possible. Lyle, the businessman, told Redd about his dream which included an outside stage that was designed with the look of the entertainment area of the Roman Empire. 'The guests would surround the stage but they would be slightly elevated. Everything would be outside with a covering to block out the sun or rain. The location would be on the beach.

"'It would have bars and eating areas everywhere. Waiters, who would serve the drinks and food,' said Lyle with a big smile on his face. 'We would use waitresses, pretty young ones in grass skirts. A big fence would surround the palace. Only rich guests would be able to patronize this paradise. Flowers and plants with many colors would be used to decorate the total area. Live small animals such as beautiful birds will be in cages to present the flavor of the Bahamas,' said Lyle.

"Redd's eyes opened wide and he said, 'Stop. I got it. My party will be on the beach.'

"'I love your idea and I know Nina will also love it. Do you know an artist that can put the ideas down on a canvas?'

"Lyle replied, 'Yes, I have it already designed in a layout; all I needed was a partner with money. A temporary stage and set-up can be put into place in three weeks tops.'

"'Oh, that is wonderful,' replied Redd. 'Nina's birthday is in three weeks and she will be twenty-one years old. It will be her party,' said Redd. 'When we met, I thought she was twenty-one but I was in love with her the moment I saw her. Nothing is too good for my love, for Nina,' said Redd.

"Redd took a second look at Lyle and realized that Lyle was a gangster, but so was he.

"Nina loved the plans but did not know the party would be for her. She was working so hard getting her part accomplished. Redd sent word to Buddy and Candee, telling them about the future plans and asking them to come to Nina's party. 'It is to be a surprise and do not breathe a word to her,' said Redd.

"The day finally came for the party and a big banner was hung: 'Welcome to Nina's Birthday Party, the Biggest and Best Party on Land.' As Nina approached the extremely large pavilion with a multi-level structure, she almost fainted, for she was truly surprised. She was turning twenty-one and it was the best day of her entire life. No one but Redd had ever loved her as much as a mother could love her child.

"'Oh my, how wonderful!' shouted Nina. She grabbed Redd, kissed him, and hugged him, and it appeared that she could not stop herself from hugging and kissing. Finally, Candee approached and said, 'Time's up. Let's get it on. Let's party.'

"The band started playing 'happy birthday' and the guests began to sing. Redd got up on stage with Nina. 'This is Nina's day and she is the love of my life. Join me in helping my wife have a birthday celebration that will be remembered by her and everyone here for many years to come. Let's toast to my wife.'

"Candee jumped up on stage and said, 'Nina is my cousin and I will make the toast to Nina and then to the newlyweds, for their union has been blessed by God. To Nina, may all your days be blessed and may God bless both of you with a long life of happiness! Okay, let's party.'

"The sky opened with hundreds of balloons falling from the beautiful sky and the band playing with popular songs from the States. The singers were gorgeous-looking; colored singers dressed to impress. She got the crowd up on their feet. People were dancing at their seats, on the dance floor, and some even jumped on top of the tables. It was a sight to see.

"Her selections along with common American Hors d'oeuvres and waitresses were sashaying around the tables, waiting on everyone with complete joy.

"It was like old times at Miller Hill in Harrisonville. Buddy and Candee were having a great time, but Buddy knew that the good times were going to come to an end soon in the near future. Therefore, he shouted out, 'Let the good times roll!'

"The sun was coming up when the last guest left. Buddy, Candee, Nina, and Redd sat at the bar just laughing and reminiscing about when they first met each other.

"Buddy recalled the day he met Redd. Buddy said, 'We were both teenagers with a future in crime. The first person I met when I entered Harrisonville was Redd. I was a runaway from some old, religious, nutty family. I could not take going to church every Sunday and that Bible study two days per week. It was killing me inside.'

"Redd said, 'My parents were great. They were true blue criminals. They were chased out of the old country, Ireland, when I was about ten. He was a bootlegger, loan shark, and had many other professions. My father was a real family man and believed in taking care of his wife and child. I am an only child and my mother died of whooping cough disease at the age of twenty-nine. When she died, my father's spirit for love of life left too.'

"'He continued to practice his profession here in Harrisonville and at the same time established himself as a real trustworthy businessman. He started his own bank, his own bar, his own gambling parlor, and his own gentlemen-and-ladies gathering place. Pop did not put up with anyone crossing him. He found ways to solve the problem. He wanted and taught me the business at an early age. I did not have any other future professional dreams but to be a criminal. Pop was great,' said Redd.

"Nina and Candee both agreed that their stories were too sad to talk about at this time but there would be plenty of time for storytelling in the future.

"The party was over and it was a big hit. That night, Redd and Nina made love for hours, over and over again. It was like this was their last great time together.

"The next day, Buddy caught up with Redd and told him they needed to talk. Over breakfast, Buddy gave Redd the bad news.

"'Redd,' said Buddy, 'I would not come home if I were you. The Feds are looking for you. One of your trusted team members was a rat. I believe I can get out of it but you and Nina are in serious trouble.'

"'They think the club and Miller Hill are totally legit and all they want is for Candee and me to pay our back taxes. They have you down for bootlegging, racketeering, murder, prostitution, and you name it. They know you are here but they cannot touch you. Please do not come home. Make this paradise your home. Please Redd, you know I love you like a brother.' He was with tears in his eyes as he spoke to Redd.

"'Buddy, I am making plans to start a club here in the Bahamas. The man that controls everything on this island helped with getting Nina's party together. His name is Lyle. Lyle is a criminal but we need him. He wants to be a partner in my new business venture,' said Redd.

"'Be careful with this Lyle. People on this island are not loyal. They just want to be rich and important,' replied Buddy.

"'Look, there is Lyle coming to our table. I will introduce him to all of you,' said Redd.

"'Good morning, Lyle,' said Redd. 'Thanks for helping me with my wife's party. It was more than I had hoped for. This is my lovely wife, Nina, her beautiful cousin, Candee, and her husband, Buddy, who is my best friend and partner,' said Redd.

"'Do your friends know of our future plans?' asked Lyle.

"'No, not yet,' replied Redd.

"'How about meeting today on the beach at about 1:00 for a beach party?' asked Lyle.

"'That sounds great,' said Candee, 'Nina and I love the beach and the ocean. We should have been born fish but were born something else,' replied Candee.

"After Lyle left, Redd said, 'I will not go back to the States. It would be crazy for me to even think about returning. Nina and I will make a life for us right here in paradise,' replied Redd.

"At 1:00, all the players were on the beach. Lyle was the last to arrive. It was obvious that he thought he was in the driver's seat with these dumb Americans. But he did not know that they were professional criminals. They had already figured him out. All they had to do was come up with a plan that would allow them to use his influence to get things moving.

"Lyle had his replica of his design for his lifelong dream of an outside paradise set-up for the Americans. He also provided project gross revenue and cost.

"Nina and Candee said, 'Let's get wet first. Eat and drink before we start talking about business.' Redd and Buddy agreed. This was also their way of slowing Lyle down, for he needed their money for this venture.

"Lyle did not get into the ocean. He neither ate nor drank anything. He just sat and waited for them. After a couple of hours, Buddy said, 'Okay, let's talk.'

"Lyle said his bid for their support for his project. The replica was very detailed with multi-levels that were designed for a full day of entertainment with beauty surrounding the compound. It consisted of five bars, five hundred tables, a large stage in the center, and three swimming pools. One pool was for the family, one for adults only, one for the general public, and several bathhouses for changing were located on the grounds of the compound. A high private fence would enclose the whole area. Food would be served all day with a large selection. The waitresses would be local pretty girls.

"After explaining the compound, Lyle said, 'Now is the time to talk turkey, like you Americans would say. What is needed is about one million to set up compound and about $500,000 to purchase food and other merchandise. With a total start-up cost of around 1.5 million,' said Lyle.

"'That's a lot of money,' replied Buddy. 'Maybe we could start small and add on as time goes on,' said Buddy.

"'Do you know what the estimated gross receipts would be on a weekly, monthly, and yearly basis?' asked Buddy.

"'Yes,' replied Lyle, 'my accountant is well known for his ability to apply past and future outcomes in the vacation industry and how it is going to grow because of increased incomes in the US. The US workers along with other countries will be looking for vacation locations to take the families. The Bahamas will be able to fulfill that need.'

"Buddy responded with confidence, 'This is a lovely spot. A person could just lose themselves here.'

"'Count me in,' said Redd.

"'Me too,' responded Buddy.

"The wives just looked at each other and said, 'It sounds like a good plan, okay.'

"Buddy and Redd agreed to give Lyle small installments of money to get things going. The first installment was to be for permits and blueprints. But first they wanted a contract with a real lawyer drawn up as to the nature and the agreement of the partnership. The ownership was to remain in the hands of Buddy and Redd, with Lyle receiving a percentage of the net income.

"Buddy and Candee returned home. They were interested in finding out who the rat was that went to the Feds about their business dealings. Candee was considered a real lady but very few people knew her real personality. She was determined to find the mole.

"She called for her accountant because he normally knew everything that was going on. Frank entered the room and started talking. 'Candee, I searched a long time to find and tried to figure out who the rat was. It finally came to me. It was our state congressman who has been indicted for corruption. My sources tell me that he struck a deal with the government about Harrisonville's illegal businesses in order to avoid jail time. They are to just give him probation.'

"'Well, you know what to do,' replied Candee. 'That testimony will never take place; make it look like a natural death,' said Candee. 'Without his testimony, they will have to drop all charges against Redd and Nina. Then they can come home where they belong. Oh, don't tell Buddy about this conversation or who the rat was,' informed Candee.

"The housekeeper who worked for the senator was on Candee's payroll. Frank told her to put rat-poisoning in the senator's dinner dessert. The senator was overweight, very unhealthy, and loved to eat rich desserts. That night, the senator had his last supper. He died about an hour after eating while he was reading a book. No one suspected anything wrong with the way he died because he looked like he was ready to keel over at any moment.

"After giving Lyle the money for the permits and architect, Redd waited a few weeks before asking Lyle for an update on the statist of the permits. Redd and Nina were having a great time in the Bahamas, but they did miss their friends and home.

"Redd received a telegram from Buddy, stating, 'If you like to come home, everything is okay because the senator was the mole and he died suddenly and all charges on Nina and you have been dropped.'

"Redd was overjoyed. As they sat for dinner that evening, Redd said to Nina, 'I have some very good news to tell you. The senator was the mole and he suddenly dropped dead. All charges have been dropped against us. If we want to go home after we get the resort up and going, we can.'

"The next day, Redd decided to find Lyle so that he could get some updates on the status of the resort project. He did not know exactly where Lyle lived but he thought that the mayor in sheriff's office would be able to help him. Redd wanted the baby to be born in Harrisonville and not the Bahamas.

"Redd entered the sheriff's office, stating, 'I need to know where the mayor lives because I have some business to talk over with him.'

"Just then, Redd looked up at the wall and saw a large photo of a well-dressed, distinguished, older gentleman. On the bottom, it gave his name and title: "Mayor."

"Redd said, 'I guess that is a picture of your mayor from past years.'

"'No,' said the officer, 'he is still living and is still the Mayor.'

"Redd reached in his pocket and pulled out a picture that was taken of Lyle and him the night of Nina's party. 'Well, do you know this man in the picture with me?' replied Redd.

"'Yes,' said the officer, 'that is the mayor's younger brother who is a bum and is always trying to make a fast buck. He lives at the mansion with the mayor's wife and family. The mayor raised him like a son when his parents died years ago.

"'Where can I find the mansion?' asked Redd.

"Redd's face became redder and he was bursting with anger. As he walked out the door, he said, 'With God as my witness, Lyle will never find another sucker.'

"Redd was extremely upset. He patted his arm to make sure his little Sue was with him. That was what he called his pistol that was strapped to his shoulder under his arm at all times. When he got dressed for the day, Sue was always part of his wardrobe.

"As he walked down the sandy street and listened to the sound of the ocean, he started thinking about the first person he had killed. He had promised himself that after killing his father's murderer, he would never kill anyone himself again.

"As he walked, he thought to himself, 'I was sixteen when I killed the man who killed my father.' After Mom died, his pop put all his energy into his business operations. One night, a man broke into their home to rob the family. Pop woke up to get a drink of water. At that time, he encountered the intruder who was his brother-in-law. The brother-in-law pulled a gun and shot Pop. 'I was given a small pistol for my birthday and Sue was used for the first time that night. Those loud noises woke me up and I grabbed my gun and walked into the room just as Pop was falling to the floor. Without speaking or thinking, I just shot my uncle. Two men were dead because of money,' thought Redd.

"'Harrisonville said I was a hero for trying to defend my father. Earlier that day, my uncle had asked Pop for a loan and he refused because he knew it was for drugs. Pop hated drugs and was totally against selling them to anyone, even to the colored people,' thought Redd.

"Finally, Redd was standing in front of the mansion with sand inside his shoes. He took off his shoes and shook out the sand. Once again he patted Sue. He knocked on the door and no one answered. Therefore, he started around the back. The sound of the ocean was beautiful and the light breeze on his face was perfect.

"He thought to himself, 'This is a perfect day for dying and today Lyle will die. No one is going to scam me and get away with it.'

"In the backyard, Lyle was sitting on the beach, drinking a margarita all by himself. Redd approached him like a gentleman. 'Hello, partner,' said Redd, 'where have you been?'

"'Looking for you,' replied Lyle.

"'I am here. Do you have the permits yet and the architect's plans for the resort yet?' asked Redd.

"'Well, I ran into a small cash problem. It is going to cost a little more,' said Lyle.

"'How much more?' asked Redd.

"'Another ten thousand will seal the deal,' replied Lyle.

"'I decided to scrap the plan and go back home. Therefore, I'd like to have my money back,' said Redd.

"Lyle stood up quickly like a big man with power and said, 'You Yankee bastard, all of you come to our island looking to get rich off of us dumb islanders. No money, no permits, and no resort, so get lost. Go home you and that bitch of a wife!' yelled Lyle.

"'You called my wife a bitch. My bitch Sue will be your bitch,' replied Redd.

"No one was around. The warm, light breeze appeared to stop and the sounds of the island had ceased. Redd took out Sue and shot Lyle in the head. He put Sue back in her resting spot and slowly walked away.

"When he returned to the hotel, he told Nina to pack her things. Redd ordered a small plane to fly them to Miami. Nina looked concerned about packing up her things and leaving quickly like two gypsies stealing away in the middle of the night. But it was not night; it was the middle of the day.

"'Redd,' said Nina, 'I am just going to leave everything; I have more of these things at home.' Redd did not reply, and that was a signal for Nina to just keep moving quickly to get herself together.

"As Nina was gathering the little bit of clothes she planned to take, she knew it was not the time to ask any questions. Therefore, she made a mental list of all the things that could have happened that would cause Redd to want to leave this beautiful paradise in such a short notice.

"Understanding Redd, Nina only had one thing on her list: murder. 'Who did he murder?' Nina was aware that Lyle had received a down payment for the resort that was being planned and that Redd was concerned about the progress and his money. Redd lived by a few rules, which were: do not mess with my woman, my money, or lie to me. If you crossed him, then your life would end quickly without much conversation.

"'Nina,' said Redd, 'that Lyle was a liar and he stole my money. I took care of him. Plus, he called you a name, and you know what happened next.'

"Nina looked at Redd and he knew he did not have to say anything else and that she was all in.

"Lyle's body was not discovered until very late that night. Lyle's family was not liked by the servants or the residents of the area. They were living large while most of the workers were poor and starving. This family was stealing all the money that was supposed to go to the people. They controlled all levels of the government. All the servants were questioned and none of them gave up any information that could help them pinpoint the murderer.

"In fact, the mayor was not told that Redd had left quickly or that Lyle and Redd had a business relationship. After a short investigation, the mayor decided that one of Lyle's girlfriends or his lowlife associates had killed him. The mayor closed the case.

As they flew back to the States, Redd thought to himself, 'I am who I am and it is what it is. I will just move on to the next part of my life; that is with my new wife that I love more than life itself.'

"The small plane landed in Miami, and Buddy and Candee were waiting for them. Buddy, with a big smile on his face, said, 'We are happy you are home. Things have not been the same without you two.' Candee seconded it with hugs and kisses.

"Buddy had a limo waiting for them and they drove off to the hotel but stopped first to eat. Buddy said to Redd that with all their criminal activities God was still providing for them, that God must have a plan but whatever it was, it would not be revealed in their lifetime.

"'What makes you say such a thing?' asked Redd.

"'Well, my friend,' said Redd. 'As you know, all charges against you have been dropped because that fat weasel of a senator died suddenly. The case against you was based on his testimony. Without him they had no case, so they had to drop

51

the charges. That was God's hand that sent him packing and caused the charges to be dropped. Next, my tax problems were solved. Nina and I only had to pay back taxes on the income from the palace. We are now solid, honest taxpayers according to the government,' said Buddy.

"As they were eating, Candee thought to herself, 'Buddy does not know the real story and that is good. He has tunnel vision. It never occurred to him that God had nothing to do with the senator's death and it was my hand that took care of the problem.

"'I guess in this case I have earned my nickname that was given to me by my true friend, Frank, the smiling assassin. Oh boy, how I love that name,' thought Candee as she quietly ate the meal with a smile.

"The next day, they drove back to Harrisonville and Redd and Buddy discussed plans for their businesses at all levels. Because of the Feds, they wanted to find a way to move away from some of their business activities.

"Redd said, 'Whatever we do, we are not getting involved in drugs. Drugs harm too many people and destroy families. Drugs will lead to the destruction of our country and I don't want to be a part of that.' Buddy agreed, and so did the ladies.

"Redd continued, 'We have the loan business which is good. How is that shaping up, Candee?'

"'Well, I had to use in a few cases an alternative method in order to get clients to pay. But I have a new system for paying. I call it the back-up plan,' said Candee.

"'How well is the back-up working?' asked Redd.

"'In fact it is the best plan that I have ever created. Frank worked with me and he has developed a good way of getting paid without ruffling up clients,' said Candee.

"'It all involves insurance; in fact, it is life insurance. Frank has a friend who is an insurance broker and with his help we are able to buy life insurance policies through various life insurance companies,' said Candee.

"'Well, I will give you a brief outline as to how it works and if you would like us to make some changes, it can be done,' said Candee.

"'In order for us to make a loan to a client, they must agree to take out a life insurance policy. Loans start at $100,000.00 with the usual interest rate. Interest and principal are paid weekly. If they miss a payment, the interest due becomes part of the principal. As you know that has always been part of the system. What is new is the insurance. All policies start at $100,000.00 with one of the four of us being the beneficiary on a client's policy.

"'If a client misses payments and his balance is catching up with the face value of the insurance, we lay out his options. We have many plans for our clients that do not involve any force. In almost every case, the back payments are paid. We don't break legs or do any bodily harm. We just have them to die of a heart attack. We want to keep them alive, for the small loans are our bread and butter. We want them to keep coming back for additional loans. They are our customers. There are other small details but this is the big picture. Also, we don't pay taxes on life insurance,' said Candee with a big smile on her face.

"'Buddy, what about the gaming operation?' asked Redd.

"'It is alive and well. Nothing has changed except that the sheriff is a regular and some of the officers too. They love the Gentlemen's Basement and the liquor. Their favorite is our local brew, moonshine. It's cheap and good. Best-kept secret in the South,' said Buddy.

"'How is our country club?' asked Nina. Buddy and Candee looked at each other and then Buddy said, 'That is a problem. Mitchell, our partner, is complaining that his business has dropped because of the palace and his only customers are old farts who just want to golf. His dinning and catering side of the business might have to close. He blames us for the decline of his family business which has serviced the community for over sixty years,' said Buddy.

"'Mitchell has been very depressed and looks like he needs to be on medication. The word is out that his young, beautiful wife has left him and the bank is going to foreclose on the club and his home,' said Candee.

"'We cannot give him any more money,' said Redd.

"'Do we have an insurance policy on him?' asked Nina.

"'Yes, we do. It is for $200,000.00 and Buddy is the beneficiary,' replied Candee.

"'Should we get rid of him before he does something stupid?' asked Redd.

"'Yes,' said Candee.

"'Make it happen soon,' replied Buddy.

"By the middle of the week, they were all home. Everything was back to normal.

"Redd was making and selling his moonshine as fast as his workers could produce the corn. The stiles were running day and night. Sales were up and so was production.

"Candee and Frank were both working closely together. Frank loved Candee but could not let her know about his feelings for her. He knew if Buddy found out, one of them would have to die. They ran the bank very well as professionals with no serious problems. The clients understood Candee and Frank were not the kind of people you would want to cross.

"Nina was running her Gentlemen's Club with an increase in demand.

"Buddy was very concerned about Mitchell and decided to have him taken care of the next day. Buddy decided to pay Mitchell a visit to just make sure it was necessary. As Buddy approached the front door, Mitchell opened the door with a shotgun in his hand, shouting, 'You dirty bastard! You destroyed my life and my business. I hope you go to hell!' Without much warning, he shot Buddy in the head and then put the gun up to his chin and took his life. 'What a day! What a day!" said Lola.

"Buddy was Mitchell's beneficiary, but Candee was the contingent beneficiary. Candee also had $200,000.00 policy on Buddy. Candee collected on both policies. Candee became very sick for about a few months. She could not keep anything down. Everyone believed it was because of Buddy's death," said Lola.

"Redd was so upset; he appeared to have gone mad. At Buddy's funeral, Redd was asked to say a few words. Redd looked into the faces of the people who had come to see Buddy for the last time. 'Buddy was my friend since we were sixteen years old,' said Redd. He lived the life that God had mapped out for him. At the age of twenty-nine, he was taken away. May God have mercy on his soul! Thank you for coming,' said Redd.

"Redd shut down all their businesses. It was hard for him to even get out of bed. Nina tried to encourage him to keep up his strength and eat," said Lola.

"Candee was feeling so bad that she thought she was also dying. Finally, Nina convinced her to go to her doctor. After the exam, the doctor came into the room and said, 'You are not dying. You are pregnant.'

"Candee could not believe it. She kept shouting, 'Me, me, me! I lost Buddy, but God has given me a baby. Thank you, thank you!' shouted Candee.

"Nina was happy for Candee. She knew that having children would not happen for her. Nina was a diabetic and getting pregnant could most likely kill her. She went to many doctors looking for help but all of them gave the same prognosis," said Lola.

Ted looked at Lola's lips and thought they were perfect. Even without lip gloss or lipstick, they had a natural light pink color. Her nose was shaped like a perfect mold on her face. 'She is beautiful,' he was thinking to himself as he tried to concentrate on Lola's words.

"Redd, with everything shut down, decided to reorganize, which included a review of all businesses and how they are run. He wanted everything to be legal. Redd wanted a future for his wife and family that was without crime," said Lola.

"Redd did not know that Nina was told not to have children because of her diabetes. Nina made a decision to get pregnant and have a family like Candee," said Lola.

"Redd reorganized and shut down everything but the palace and the Gentlemen's Basement. The palace was a place that he could have fun at and enjoy himself and relax," said Lola.

'With Buddy out of the picture, Frank was encouraged to confess his love to Candee," said Lola.

"As Frank was taking Candee home from the doctor's clinic, he said the following, 'Candee, I have loved you from the day I set eyes on you but you and Buddy looked like a couple that God had blessed. I want to marry you and raise your child as my own. Do you think that is possible?'

"'Frank, only if you take me away from all this criminal activity today. I want my baby to live an honest life and work for an honest day's pay. I don't want to worry about an enemy walking up to my baby and shooting him in the head. God has given me a chance to live a Christian life. Will you change your ways and become a born-again Christian?' asked Candee.

"'Yes,' responded Frank, 'I was hoping that we could leave and start over. We should say goodbye to our friends and not tell anyone where we are going. In fact, I do not know where we are going. We have plenty of money and can live a good life with each other no matter where we call home. I could open up my own accounting firm and you could work with me if you want,' replied Frank.

"Candee replied, 'Let's go for it.'

"Candee rushed to find Nina and tell her the news. As she approached the house, the front door was open and Candee went in, yelling, 'Nina, Nina!' As she ran through the rooms, there was no sign of Nina. Finally, as she passed the bathroom, that is where she found Nina," stated Lola.

"Nina was crying because she wanted to get pregnant but there was a health situation that might keep her from having the baby or living long enough to raise the baby. Nina was pregnant and now she would have to make a decision about whether to try to have the baby. Candee or Redd did not know about her health, so she decided not to tell them. She believed if she told them about her health, they would try to get her to terminate the pregnancy," stating Lola.

"Nina said, 'I am pregnant. I just left the doctor's clinic.'

"'That's good, right,' responded Candee.

"'Yes,' replied Nina, 'but I don't know if Redd will want a family this soon after Buddy's death.'

"'I guarantee you that he will be extremely happy about being a father,' said Candee.

"'Nina, call Redd and have him to come home,' said Candee.

"Redd came home, and Frank and Nina wanted their best friends to hear their good news first," said Lola.

"'We are leaving Harrisonville right now. Here are the deeds to all our real estate. I have signed everything over to both of you. I want my baby to live a normal life. Frank and I are going to get married. This is Buddy's baby and Frank will be his father. We love the two of you but we want to leave this town and this life behind us,' said Candee.

"'Now Nina,' said Candee, 'it is your turn.'

"Nina looked straight into Redd's eye and said, 'I am pregnant.'

"Redd shouted, 'Wonderful!'

"'Our babies will hopefully meet up with each other one day. That is very good news for all of us. New family members and new beginnings,' said Frank.

"'Well, we are off, hitting the road to nowhere. If you ever need us, put an ad in the N.C Journal. We will have it delivered to us no matter where we live. Use 'Harris' as the code,' said Candee.

"As the months flew by, Nina was totally bedridden. She would not allow the doctor to tell Redd about her condition. The doctor informed Nina that she had less than fifty percent chance of survival during the delivery of the babies," said Lola.

"All during that time, Candee and Frank never tried to contact Nina or Buddy. Their names were never mentioned. That part of their past was gone forever," said Lola.

"Your past is never gone. It is with you all your life and it will show up in future generations. I truly believe that about the past. We can't change the past, but we can learn a valuable lesson from it," said Ted.

"On the day Nina went into labor, she had to have a C-Section and she died on the delivery table," said Lola.

"She died," said Ted, with a surprised and stunning look on his face. "She never got to see the babies?" asked Ted.

"Coming out of the delivery room, Redd stopped the doctor, stating, 'How are my wife and the baby?'

"'Sorry, she did not make it. We only gave her less than a fifty-percent chance of surviving the delivery,' informed the doctor. 'The babies are very healthy. With all her problems, she did take good care of the babies,' said the doctor.

"'What do you mean with all her medical problems?' asked Redd.

"'Your wife did not tell you even at the end,' responded the doctor.

"'Tell me what?' said Redd.

"'She was a diabetic and she was told not to ever get pregnant because she might not survive the delivery. She was strong and if it had only been one baby, her chances would have been better. Her heart and kidneys failed her and caused a heart attack,' said the doctor.

"Redd looked down at Nina and said, 'I will never love any woman like I loved you. The short time we were together was wonderful and I am thankful. Goodbye, my love,' with tears flowing downs his face as he covered her face with the white sheets and walked out.

"As he looked into the nursery, he saw the two babies, two boys that looked just like Nina, both with black curly hair and beautiful. 'What should I call them? I want them to have their mother's initials,' he said, thinking to himself.

"'Nickolas and Nathan, that's it, and your mother will be proud of the two of you someday,' said Redd, talking out loud to himself.

"After coming home from the palace and not having Nina with him, it made Redd withdraw from his friends. The day the babies were picked up, Redd had no idea of how to be a parent and how to care for the two identical twins that were given to him by God.

"Therefore, the nurse at the hospital gave him the name of an older lady whose husband had died and her children were grown and she needed something to keep her busy," said Lola.

"It was the answer to his prayers, for this lady took good care of the boys. Redd sent them to a private school because he wanted the best for the two of them.

"Redd kept the moonshine business going and the palace and the Gentlemen's Basement. Many of the big shots hung out at Redd's place. All three businesses were alive and well. Business was better than ever. Redd was one of the best repeated clients at the Gentlemen's Basement. He had all kinds of liquor but loved his moonshine," said Lola.

"The women were running after Redd but he only wanted one thing from them. That was to make love with them as if it was Nina. Some of the women realized this but thought he might fall in love with them. But that never happened," said Lola.

"One night, Redd came home from the palace and Ida, the housekeeper, was lying on the kitchen floor. She was dead. The doctors said she died of a heart attack. The boys were older, around eight years old. The boys were big enough to help around the house and the farm. Redd had dreams for them; he wanted to them to go to college and become honest businessmen. He also wanted them to understand how to protect and take care of their business," said Lola.

"With all that was going on with Redd, he needed help. Shortly after Ida died, a little young girl of about nineteen years old knocked on his door, stating, 'I am looking for work. I just moved here last week and the operator at the boarding home in town said that you might need some help with the kids and housekeeping,' said the young girl.

"Thinking to himself, Redd looked her over. She was cute, but not his Nina.

"After a few seconds, Redd said, 'Come in and let's talk.' Rita started working that day and Redd liked her a lot, but she was not Nina," said Lola.

"Rita and Redd became an item. Folks sometimes referred to her as Mrs. Redd. And she would reply, 'Not yet.'

"One day out of the blue, Redd came home early, stating, 'Rita, I need to talk to you. I am getting older and the boys are men and I need a wife. Will you marry me?' asked Redd.

"Rita, looking shocked, said, 'Yes.'

"Rita knew her marriage to Redd was not going to be the same as it was when he had Nina but she was ready to settle for second place. Rita was at least hoping for a big wedding but Redd wanted to just go to the justice of the peace and got married, so that is what happened," said Lola.

"As the years passed by, the boys were getting older and they started hanging around with Redd. They would listen and hang on to every word he spoke. They loved their father and wanted to be just like him. He had learned over the years to be a fair man but if you crossed him, you would pay the price," said Lola.

"The boys were smart in every way, that is, street-smart and book-smart. They learned how to work the farm and how to manage the palace very quickly. In fact, they had some ideas to run past Redd. When it came time for them to go off to college, Redd was happy but sad at the same time. He loved the boys and would miss having them around. But at the same time he wanted them to get quality education. They both got scholarships from the same university and off they went," said Lola.

"Lola, did they ever try to contact Candee to let them know that Nina had died?" asked Ted.

"No, Redd said that he wanted to let them have a clean break from the past."

"So all those years passed and they never heard from them again?" said Ted.

"That's right, never again. Candee and Frank were only in their late twenties and had plenty of time to change their life and to start over again," said Lola.

"After the boys went away to college, what did Redd do?" asked Ted.

"Redd got totally involved with the palace and his moonshine sales. Moonshine was very popular in the South. It was cheap and easy to get. Redd did not pay any taxes or fees connected to moonshine. With the blue laws in some of the northern states, moonshine at Sunday speakeasies was very profitable even in the South," said Lola.

"The twins were very popular at the college. They were popular for several reasons. They were making and selling moonshine in the woods near the school and having poker games on Saturday nights. They were very smart and both were majoring in business. These subjects and the material came very easy to them. In fact, they were in the top five percent of their class," said Lola.

"Even some of the staff at the college became regular customers. Because they were very good-looking, the girls were chasing after them. They had the charm and looks of Nina and the business sense of Redd. They were not running these businesses because they needed the money but because they saw opportunity and it was in the genes.

"The boys informed their father about their business activities and Redd told him to stop making moonshine and that he would make deliveries in suitcases once a month. Redd did not want them to get caught making the liquor and get kicked out of school," said Lola.

"Nick and Nate were so good at selling moonshine that Redd wanted to expand in other colleges. During spring breaks, the twins would sell to Greek fraternities for their houses and beach parties. The distribution system that was set up was well organized with colleges in the South and the North as far as New York," said Lola.

"'By the time we graduated, we will have plenty of money to go legit,' said Nick.

"'Our future partners are chemistry majors and have shown me figures that suggest that biofuels will be the thing of the future. We are only in our early twenties, and if we start developing our product now, the biofuel market will be ours. Pop's generation did whatever they had to do to make it. Now it is our turn to do it our way,' said Nick.

"Nick and Nate were alike in many ways but also different in many ways. Nick wanted to go legit. On the other hand, Nate secretly loved the criminal life. That lifestyle gave him power and influence over others," said Lola.

"Not long after graduation, they returned home and worked the college operation from the farm but they could not grow enough corn to keep up with demand. So, Nick called on his chemistry friend to develop an additive to put in the liquor in order to increase the supply. The friend came up with an additive which proved to be wonderful. Production was back on track," said Lola.

"Rita worked hard, taking care of the house and cooking for Redd and the boys. Redd was spending most of his time at the palace, especially the Gentlemen's Basement. Rita was not getting attention. Many people wondered why she stayed with Redd. Deep down inside, she loved him and was willing to do anything to just be with him," said Lola.

"The moonshine competitor that Redd had killed was Rita's oldest brother. Rita never knew her brother, for he left home a few years after she was born. There was fifteen years' difference in their ages. She never told anyone that he was her brother. Her brother was looked upon by the community as the lower class in Harrisonville. She had status and money and influence which she thought was enough," said Lola.

"Thinking to herself, Rita said, 'I have cleaned this house, cooked his meals, and raised his boys, and what do I have to show for all these years? Now he has killed my brother.'

"Rita quietly drank a few glasses of moonshine and sat in the dark living room, waiting for Redd to come home. The longer she sat, the more she drank," said Lola.

"Rita fell asleep and when she woke up, Redd was in the bed fast asleep. She picked up Sue (his handgun), walked right over to him, and pointed the gun to his head, stating, 'Nina is gone and now you can go with her.' One shot to the head killed him. Then she put Sue under her chin and pulled the trigger. And that was the end of that generation of criminals," said Lola.

"Oh my, oh my!" looking stunned, Ted was lost for words.

"Nick and Nate closed down the palace for the night and came home. As they entered the house, they could smell the strange odor of death in the air. The house was completely dark and totally calm and quiet," said Lola.

"Walking slowly through the house, they called out for Rita and Redd but no one responded. Finally, they turned on the lights in Redd's bedroom and there they were, lying in pools of blood. Their faces were not recognizable. It was like looking at two monsters," said Lola.

"'Nick, call the sheriff,' said Nate.

"When the sheriff got to the house, he could not believe what he saw. 'Do you know why she killed Redd?' asked the sheriff.

"'There are no notes or indication that they were arguing,' said Nick.

"'Well boys, this is a tragedy and a devastating loss for Harrisonville. Nothing will ever be the same,' said the sheriff.

"'What should we do, sheriff?' asked Nate.

"'Gather up everything that you want and any papers that are important. After you have secured your things, set the house on fire. It is better for the community to remember these two as a loving couple. I will make a statement that they died in the fire and could not get out,' said the sheriff.

"Within about an hour, the two boys had cleared the house of its entire valuables and set the house on fire," said Lola.

"'Nate,' said Nick, 'Pop had plans for us, but I have my own plans. I want to go legit. We have plenty of money and we are the heirs of all his assets. He also has an insurance policy for $2,000,000 with the two of us as the beneficiaries. I also would like to try my hand at law school. I would like to have my own law firm someday,' said Nick.

"Nick continued, 'My chemistry friends have convinced me that biofuels will be a cleaner and better alternative to oil in the future. We are young and have time to invest in this alternative fuel. Our corn supply can be divided into feed for livestock, consumption, and biofuel,' said Nick.

"'Nick, I like living on the edge and it is in my genes. I am going to stay on here at Harrisonville and continue running the palace. Nothing is forever, and Pop's generation is now gone and we have to be strong and stay focused,' said Nate.

"'Let's split up his estate,' said Nick. 'You take the palace and I will take the farm. Any other real estate we will sell to the locals,' said Nick.

"On the farm, Nick and his chemistry friends designed and built a large complex with state of the art labs. In the labs, they developed better quality corn and fertilizers which enabled them to grow the crops faster. At the same time, Nick enrolled in the local university's law school.

"Nick's new life was going very well. He was an outstanding law student and entrepreneur. Using corn as a biofuel caused big concerns with producers and sellers of oil. Nick, in the back of his head, always remembered his father's plans about building an empire of businesses. Nick realized that growing corn for biofuel would be the key component of his future empire," said Lola.

"Nate was busy reorganizing the banking system, gaming hall, and the palace in order to modernize their systems. He loved criminal activities. It was in his genes. But before he reopened in full force, he wanted to have a memorial for his father and Rita. Nick felt that there should be closure on the old generation so that the new generation could start over without any regrets," said Lola.

"The memorial was held at the palace. Many politicians, law officers, and friends attended. Frank and Candee did not come. Nick and Nate had heard stories about Frank and Candee but had never met them. Nick found a note written by Candee, stating, 'If you ever need us, put an ad in the NC Journal and we will come.' Nick put the ad in, but they did not show up," said Lola.

"At the memorial, Nick and Nate spoke. Nick said the following: 'My mother, Nina, and my father were in love. My mother died having my brother and me in the name of love. My father loved her from the first time he saw her. Now they are together. May God have mercy on their souls!'

"Nick and Nate knew what Rita did and her name was not mentioned at the memorial. No pictures of her were displayed. All the pictures were of Nina and

Grandpa," said Lola.

"When the memorial was over, everyone was invited to the opening of the new palace. In fact the name had changed to 'Palace Grande.' A big banner across the entrance stated: 'Nina and Redd, you will be missed,' said Lola.

"As you walked in, a live band and singers were getting it on. All the tables were decorated with pretty flowers, just as if Nina and Candee had fixed the tables.

"A waiter greeted everyone at the door and escorted them to a table. A different set of waiters took their drink order which was on the house. A third set of waiters walked around with Hors d'oeuvres. After almost all the tables were filled, a long row of all types of foods was uncovered. A dance floor was designed to hold a great number of dancers at the same time. Nate had remodeled the whole building. Even the Gentlemen's Basement was grander," said Lola.

"Nate and Nick were sitting at the bar and a tall, beautiful, young lady walked through the door. She had long coal-black hair, skin that was the color of pure cream, and bright green eyes. She was dressed in a slim red dress that curved with her body. She looked like she just stepped out of Vogue magazine," said Lola.

"Nate could not take his eyes off her. She stopped and looked around and then headed straight for the bar. As she approached, Nate started sweating and taking deep breaths. It took her a long time to make it to the bar because she moved very slowly as if she was auditioning for a part in a movie. This beauty had all the right moves. It was obvious that she was a professional at whatever it was that she did. At some point, she was standing in front of Nate," said Lola.

"'Hello boys,' she said, 'you look like twins. Double trouble, I see. I have been traveling all night and most of the day. How about buying a lady a drink? Make that a margarita?' she said, sipping on her drink. 'This appears to be a nice place to work. Do you know if they are hiring?'

"Nate, without hesitating, said, 'Yes.'

"Nick said, 'Wait, what are your skills?'

"'Guys, I can do everything. I can dance, sing, play the piano, bartend, and wait on customers. I am a complete package,' she said.

"'Well,' said Nick, 'that's the easy thing. Can you cook?'

"'Sir, I told you, I can do everything. Cooking is my middle name.' She smiled as she responded.

"'Okay, dance with me. I have dreamed of a girl who can do everything,' said Nate.

"'Touching her body is like touching an angel that just fell out of the sky from heaven, as they slow-danced to Etta James' song. 'At Last,' thought Nate.

"As they were dancing, Nate asked, 'What is your name?'

"'My name is Zola,' she responded.

"'That sounds like music to my ears,' said Nate.

"Zola and Nate are my parents. They are criminals of the second generation," said Lola.

"Zola was from New Orleans. She was part French and part black. She was considered Creole. She looked white but was not hundred percent. Many of her family members on her mother's side were dark-skinned blacks. She never tried to act white; she was just herself," said Lola.

"After dancing, Nick wanted to see her sing and play the piano. Without hesitation, he jumped on the baby grand and shouted, 'Let's roll!'

"After a few notes, she started singing Fats Domino's song, 'Blueberry Hill.' Everyone who could get up started dancing. The whole Palace Grande was singing with her. If they could not get on the dance floor, they stood on top of the tables. When the song was over, they yelled for more. It seemed as if she played all night. She was enjoying herself. She played and sang her favorites, which appeared to be everyone else's favorites too. I'm in love again, I'm walkin', walking to New Orleans, and ain't it a shame? Zola, all by herself, brought Boogie Woogie to a little county town like Harrisonville. That was my mother, the girl that could do everything," said Lola.

"Nick looked at Nate and shook his head, for he knew his brother would be okay, and walked out," said Lola.

"Zola went home with Nate and claimed him for herself that night. She was nineteen years old but looked and acted older and Nate was twenty-six years old. They both loved each other. Within a few weeks, they were married.

"Zola was from New Orleans and wanted to bring her hometown to Harrisonville. Nate wanted to reorganize and it was the right time to make the changes. Zola's layout included an outside component during spring and summer, with Bar-B-Q being cooked outside on large pit, clams on the half shell, corn on cob, greens, all types of salads, and a large bar. Tables with umbrella would surround the live band and singers.

"Inside would be several bars with beautiful, decorated tables with a DJ. On the inside, the tables would be beautifully decorated with waiters to take the orders with a full menu. Zola had suggested that they be opened just on Friday, Saturday, and Sunday. This way, they would have the rest of the week for planning and relaxation.

"In the plans, Zola wanted a large swimming pool so that the whole family could enjoy the Palace Grande. Nate loved the plans. Within a short period of time, they were up and running. Zola was the major entertainment attraction on Saturday night. She played the piano, sang, and danced to the local band. She was a big hit on and off the stage.

"Zola knew that at some point she would have to tell Nate that she was not totally white. She did not know how he would feel. So she decided not to tell right away."

Ted looked at Lola and said, "You are not white."

"No, not totally," replied Lola.

"My grandmother on my mother's side was black and we have a rainbow of colors in our family which makes it a fun family to be associated with. We have never tried to pass for white. We marry people that we love and not because of the color of their skin. My mother said it was the color of a person's heart that counts and not the color of their skin," said Lola.

"That is the only reason a person should marry, for love. My grandparents married for love. Their love for each other is what got them through the hard times so that they could enjoy the good time. That is what I want for my wife and me one day," said Ted.

"The Gentlemen's Basement and the gambling hall were opened every night. That area was remodeled, and it had its own adult exercise room and swimming pool, bar, and, restaurant. It was totally separate from the rest of the complex. After a few years, Zola decided that they should add a few amusements for the kids. The surrounding area put up hotels to accommodate outside visitors. Harrisonville had become a vacation spot for couples and families.

"Back in New Orleans, my grandparents controlled the whole area. They controlled all the drugs, liquor sales, gambling, and prostitution activities. They were people that you did not want to cross. If you did, you would end up in the swamp.

"People feared them. They even had the police force and government officials on their payroll. Visitors to New Orleans could eat, drink, gamble, dance, and have a good time. New Orleans is where Zola learned how to do almost everything.

"Singing and playing the piano came naturally to her. On the weekends, she would visit The Hill, her parents' club, and entertain the customers. One night at the club, my mother was high off of marijuana and just finished playing and singing. She was on her way home when a man grabbed her and tried to rape her and she pulled out a knife and stabbed him over and over. With blood all over herself, she went back to the club. Her parents cleaned her up and gave her money and a ticket out of town and that is how she ended up in Harrisonville.

"The man she killed was a police officer. Being the type of business people they were, her father thought it would be better for her to leave and let the murder go unsolved. One of the workers at the club heard the conversation between my grandparents and my mother and decided to blackmail my grandparents. Well, he ended up in the swamp.

"In previous years, my grandparents were in a drug war with two other drug cartels: The Brotherhood of N.O. and the Blood Brothers who controlled most of the wards, and they were uneducated and did not understand how to stay in business. The Brotherhood was a white cartel and the Blood Brothers were black. They were always having wars and coming to my grandparents for help.

"In many cases, it was for large sums of money. The cartel would have to give something as a guarantee in case the repayment was late or not repaid. Territory or customers were the most common forms of repayment. With the ongoing cartel wars and the loans, these two cartels were put out of business and my grandparents moved in and took over. They controlled everything.

"Any small business in the area had to buy insurance from them. This insurance allowed them to operate without fear of being robbed or the police harassing their business. Every month, a collector would stop by the business and pick up the cash. All fees were the same.

"My grandparents were professional gangsters. They owned the police department, most of the clubs and bars, rooming houses, and controlled horse-racing tracks, and gaming tables for poker. My grandfather was the best when it came to playing poker. In fact, that is how he acquired his first bar, playing poker. He won the club from a lady who had relocated to New Orleans from Philadelphia. She was good but did not know that he was a card shark who did not like losing. Winning the club was the beginning of his building of his criminal empire. After that, acquiring other establishments and buying influence became easy.

"Therefore, my mother grew up in an environment of lawlessness and crime. Nate did not know much about my mother but he loved her, and her background would not have made any difference.

"Mom and Dad had been married for about two years when she became pregnant. Mom knew it was time to tell Dad that she was part black. Her ability to cook came from her mother's side of the family. As a small child, she was taught how to cook food in the New Orleans' style. Zola became an outstanding cook.

One night when the Palace Grande was closed, she cooked a fantastic dinner and got dressed in her sexiest dress and waited for Nate to come home. Her mom had always told her that the way to a man's heart was through his stomach.

"Zola heard Nate coming and she rushed to the door. 'Hello, honey,' said Zola. 'I have several treats for you tonight.'

"Nate looked at her and smiled, 'I surrender, and I know I am all yours tonight. So, let's eat; it smells great,' said Nate.

"'Nate,' said Zola, 'I have a few things to tell you. First, my parents are not legit business people. I don't know how to say this, so I will just tell it like it is. They are gangsters. They control all of New Orleans and beyond. I am part black; my mother is what they called Creole, half French and half black. Next, I am pregnant with twins,' she said, looking relieved as she looked Nate straight in his eye.

"Nate was not surprised about her background but overwhelmed with joy about the babies. 'Nina, oh I mean Zola, my twin brother, as you know, is a lawyer. He looked into your background years ago before we got married. I know all about your mother and father. I also know why you landed in Harrisonville. Nick said that the two families were a perfect fit, family partners in crime, and our babies will be beautiful, just like their mother,' said Nate.

"Nick heard about the good news and wanted to tell them in person how happy he was for the two of them. The next day, he stopped for dinner and it was a wonderful dinner – Louisiana-style chicken, rice and beans, collard greens, and sweet potatoes. Zola was right; she was an excellent cook.

Holding up a glass of red wine, Nick said, 'You two are my best friends; I will always be there for you.'

"At that point, Nate said, 'We want you to be the Godfather of the twins. You are living a legit life and in our business. Life can be short. Therefore, we want you to raise our kids if anything happens to us. Can we count on you?'

"Without hesitation, Nick said, 'Thank you, it will be a pleasure.' I will always look out for them whether you are alive or have passed away.'"

Ted said to Lola, "Your defense is very creditable. I believe we have a slam-dunk defense. Tomorrow you will go before the judge and he will ask you how you plead. You will say not-guilty. Then I will say not-guilty because of mental disease, mental defect, and extreme family criminal environment. They produced a lifestyle that was considered normal in your family. If your mother's family was anything like your father's family, you would have been off the hook. Tomorrow is a big day. Try to get some sleep. Court starts at nine and I will be on time. I will ask if you can be released on your own recognition. This is your first offense and you should be released with a small bail. I know the prosecutor. He is fair.

He is an old man and I heard some stories about his parents that question his early life growing up in a family that has a bad family background. This might help our case."

Lola walked into court looking very stunning. Her hair was pulled up and even though she had very little makeup on, she was still beautiful. With tears in her eyes, she said, "Not-guilty."

Ted told the judge the reason behind her not-guilty plea. The prosecutor was shocked by the reason and just remained silent for a few minutes. To Ted's surprise, the prosecutor agreed to release her with a small bail.

Ted said to Lola, "Do you know the prosecutor?"

"No, but maybe he knows my family," responded Lola.

"He has always been fair, but not that fair," said Ted.

When Lola got home, Ted came in and said, "Okay, let's get back to your defense."

Lola had no problem getting back to her defense.

"My Uncle Nick's life was full of excitement. His farm and bio-lab was shaping up very well. He had developed several types of special corn. None of the types used much water but produced quicker and larger crops. Twenty-five percent of the corn harvest was for consumption, thirty-five percent for feed, and forty percent for biofuels. The farm in upstate PA was used strictly for biofuels," said Lola.

"One day as he sat on his big porch in Harrisonville, a well-dressed man drove up in a limo and asked to speak to Nick.

"'I am Nick,' he responded.

"'The waste from your bio-lab is contaminating the soil and water in the PA area. You will have to stop your experiments and production,' said the man.

"'Who are you?' asked Nick.

"'I represent groups of individuals that are in the oil business. We have purchased almost all the facilities that are producing biofuels. We'd like to buy your farm. Here's my card. Call me when you are ready to talk,' said the man.

"The card said, 'Harry Jones, Special Services – 888-235-9080.'

"'Sorry, but I am not selling,' said Nick.

"'You will,' responded the man.

"Nick realized that his biofuels were driving the price of oil down. He had received a nice letter from the EPA, praising him for his dedication with respect to the environment. All his testing was within the guidelines of the EPA.

"Nick worked hard every day like a drug addict, trying not to become a criminal like one could become in the environment that he was raised in. But that situation could possibly cause him to lose control.

"Nick called Nate and told him what was going on. Nate said, 'Nick, I am coming to PA with a few of my best helpers and we will guard the farm.'

"When they arrived, workers told them that some men had come by and told them "to leave, for they might find themselves in the ashes." Nate patted his shoulder to see if his father's gun was still there. Sue was reliable. If he needed her, she was ready for action.

"That night, the men worked shifts in order to keep an eye on the lab and corn fields. Nick said to Nate, 'Maybe you should sell the farm. It is not worth anyone getting hurt. Tomorrow we can go put a complaint in with the local police department. If they do not help, we can call the State Police, okay?'

"That next morning, the boys when to the police office and told them the situation. Nick pulled out the man's business card. 'Special services,' said the sheriff. 'We will see how special he is when I lock him up for terroristic threats,' said the sheriff.

"Nick called Mr. Jones and he set up a meeting for that Friday. What Mr. Jones did not know was that the sheriff would be at the meeting. The meeting took place and the boys told Mr. Jones that under no circumstances were they selling the farm. The sheriff reminded Mr. Jones that this was their final answer."

Ted asked, "Did anything ever happen to the farm, Lola?"

"Not right away but it became a problem later," responded Lola.

"That Mr. Jones had the law officers on his side. That day at the farm was a sham to make it look like things were going to be okay. But every week, Nick was getting something in the mail from the county about some made-up violation. On various occasions, a township inspector would come out and complain about something. Nick was getting tired of the harassment and called Nate.

"'Nate,' said Nick, 'let's sell everything in PA and Harrisonville and move out of state.'

"'Zola is pregnant with twins and I don't know if she wants to move at this moment. I will ask her,' said Nate.

"Zola was seven-and-a-half months pregnant but was still working hard at the Palace Grande. That night, Nate said to Zola, 'Nick wants to sell everything and move out of state and start over. It sounds like a good idea. It is all up to you.'

"'I believe it will be the best thing for all of us, twins included,' responded Zola.

"'I have only one request. I want to move back to New Orleans,' said Zola.

"'That sounds good to me and I know it will be fine with Nick,' responded Nate.

"When my brother and I were born, my Uncle Nick said we were the prettiest babies that he had ever seen. Basically, that is how our family and friends felt too," said Lola.

"I looked white but my brother took after my mother's ancestors. He was light brown, with black hair that he cut very short, tall, and with brown eyes," said Lola.

"Both boys understood their father's plans for them, but they had their own plans. Nick said to Nate, 'I want to practice law, get married, have a bunch of children, live on a boathouse, and make honest money. We are millionaires. Why put ourselves through this horror every day?'

"Nate lowered his head and said, 'It is in my blood. It was in our grandfather, our father, and now I have a wife and in-laws who can never get enough power, influence, or money to be satisfied. Sorry brother, but that is the way the cookie crumbled.'

"Nick opened up a law office and Nate joined forces with Eddie and Ella, his in-laws. Together they were untouchable," said Lola.

"New Orleans was sin city. Nick opened up his law office in the heart of downtown. He made up his mind that he would interview potential clients and if he believed they were innocent, he would represent them. That sounded good until a great-looking lady walked into his office. Nick could not take his eyes off her.

"As Nick was standing up to greet her, he felt that before she gave her story as to why she needed a lawyer, she was guilty. He could see it in her beautiful, bright blue eyes.

"'My name is Eva Johns and I need a good lawyer,' she said.

"'The police told me I needed a lawyer,' she said.

"'Start from the beginning and tell me your story,' responded Nick.

"'My boyfriend, who was really my sugar daddy, was beating me up and I felt like he was going to kill me. So I reached over and grabbed his gun off the nightstand and shot him three times. This happened last night. The police took pictures of me. I went to the hospital and the doctor said I have brushed ribs, a concussion, and bruises on my hips,' said Eva.

"'What is the name of the deceased?' asked Nick.

"'His name is Eddie,' responded Eva.

"'The Eddie who is the most powerful man in New Orleans?' said Nick.

"Yes, that is my sugar daddy,' responded Eva.

"'Let's go get a drink at my place,' said Nick.

"When they got to Nick's apartment, Eva started crying, stating, 'I don't know how I got myself mixed up in such a mess. I am a college-graduate student working on a paper about underworld crime bosses. I had to play the part in order to get the story.

"'About a year ago, I went to the club knowing that he would be there. It was known that he was a sucker for young, good-looking women. For some reason, his wife always turned the other way and acted like business as normal. Nothing seemed to bother her, and as time went by, we became lovers. He trusted me with many of his secret dealings,' said Eva.

"'I don't know if I will be able to take your case. Eddie is my twin brother's father-in-law. They are partners. But there is a law firm down the street that is very good and they have a reputation of getting good results in cases like yours. I will call them in the morning for you. For now, why don't you go into my bedroom and get a good night's sleep? We can talk more in the morning,' said Nick.

"The next morning, Eva was up early and was making breakfast. 'Good morning, Nick,' said Eva. 'I feel better today. I hope that law firm takes my case. I have very little money but will work to pay them,' said Eva.

"'I will help you,' responded Nick. He did not truly believe her story, but he could not determine what she was hiding. Nick called Stevenson Law Firm and spoke to Mr. Stevenson. He had read about Eddie's death in the local newspaper.

"Stevenson wanted Nick to bring her over that afternoon. Nick was feeling very good and found himself attracted to Eva. He loved the way she walked, her hair, her body, and the way she talked. Eva was also attracted to Nick.

"Mr. Stevenson said to Nick, 'You are from Harrisonville, N.C., I understand. My parents lived there for several years but moved to New Orleans before I was born. That was long before your time.'

"'Yes, I was born in Harrisonville,' responded Nick.

"'What brings you to New Orleans?' asked Mr. Stevenson.

"'My twin brother's in-laws live here. In fact, Eddie was my brother's father-in-law,' said Nick.

"'Well, they're complicated things and I want you to leave, and don't tell anyone that you came here with Eva. Her defense will be between her and her legal team,' responded Mr. Stevenson.

"As Nick was leaving, he was thinking to himself. 'I think this lawyer knows something about my family that he is hiding from me. Maybe he does not want to embarrass me in front of Eva or maybe it is personal.'

"'Eva, I can get you off but you will have to tell me the truth. Not some of the truth but all of it,' said Mr. Stevenson.

"'My father worked for Eddie and Ella as their bookkeeper. One day when I was only a teenager, my father went missing. Later, his body was found in the swamp. My mother died with a broken heart. Before she died, she told me that Eddie's daughter left town because she killed a police officer. My father found out about the murder and was blackmailing Eddie and he had him killed. When I went away to college, I changed my name and vowed to get revenge for my father's murder and my mother's broken heart,' said Eva.

"'You know that Ella is not going to let this go. She will get to you. She is worse than Eddie. She is the mastermind behind their operations. She calls all the shots,' said Mr. Stevenson.

"'I played my part very well and Eddie allowed me to be part of his daily business transactions. I have photocopies of drug transactions with clients, prostitution records with customers' names, and all the names of judges, elected officials, and law enforcement. I am an undercover agent with the FBI. Please do not blow my cover. Don't allow Nick to know who I am. I believe he is honest but his brother and the rest of the family are gangsters. I know Eddie and Ella have murdered many people including my father who was their bookkeeper.

"'With my father as their bookkeeper, he kept secret records of Eddie's everyday activities. It is in the form of a diary. My mother did not know about these records. I found them by accident. After my mother died, I was having some renovation work done because I was planning on selling the homestead. I discovered a false wall in the bathroom and when I knocked it open, I found the diary. Even the FBI doesn't know what I have. I told them that I was onto something but it was a work in process,' said Eva.

"'Eddie paid off all my college loans. In my senior year, I was recruited by the FBI and I asked to be assigned to New Orleans because I understood the people and the mentality of the culture.

"'I have been working on this case for three years. Do not tell the prosecutor this story. He is in Eddie's book. We will have to get the FBI involved,' said Eva.

"'What a story! But I have something to show you. This is my FBI badge. I am with the FBI. When you landed in my office, I knew it might be the big break I was looking for ten years,' said Mr. Stevenson.

"'What's next?' asked Eva.

"'That depends on what the diary and your records prove,' said Mr. Stevenson.

"'Okay, why was Eddie beating on you?' asked Mr. Stevenson.

"'He went to my apartment when I was not home. He pays the rent, therefore he has a key. I forgot and left a picture of my mother and father lying on my bed. That is how he figured out who I really was. The daughter of the man he killed,' said Eva.

'He was sitting in the living room in the dark with a drink in his hand when I entered the apartment. As I entered the doorway, he yelled out: you fucking bitch! I knew it was over. He asked me to verify who I really was and I told him. I also told him he was under arrest and that I was an FBI agent. He took his fist and socked me in the face and started kicking me around. He was shouting, 'You will never live to see me go to jail, you bitch!' After a few minutes of his abuse, I looked on the end of table and realized he had left his gun sitting on the table. With both eyes almost shut, I reached over and grabbed his gun and shot him several times in the head. And that is how it happened.'

"'Did you tell anyone else about what really happened?' asked Mr. Stevenson.

"'No,' responded Eva.

"'Good. If you do, we will both be dead before the sun sets today.

"'Let's get the records and take them to the bank and put them in my safe deposit box. I will give you a key in case something happens to me,' said Mr. Stevenson.

"After they got the records, Eva called Nick and asked him if she could stay with him for a while," said Lola.

"Oh boy, what a story! Let's see. Nick is your uncle, right?" asked Ted.

"That's right, and much later he married Eva. So she became my aunt. The FBI had the case transferred out of state. They knew that many of the officials in Louisiana were corrupt and could not be trusted," said Lola.

"'Nate and Zola were not in any of my records. They have only recently moved to New Orleans. Lucky for them that they were still living in Harrisonville when most of the corruption was taking place,' said Eva.

"'Nate and his wife dodged the bullet here but that family has been under investigation for many years. During the time when the father Buddy was living, he was indicted for murder but the main witness, who was a state senator, died suddenly. Charges were dropped and the case was closed. But that family has a long history of illegal activities. That generation is gone but the next generation was trained to be just like the parents. Nick is the only honest one to ever be born in that bloodline. Even the great-grandfather had criminal genes,' said Mr. Stevenson.

"Ella was so upset over Eddie being murdered by this little bitch that she put a contract out on her. Ella did not know that the FBI was involved. She called in her big guns to find out more about Eva," said Lola.

"'I want her investigated,' said Ella as she spoke to the chief of police. 'I do not have a good feeling about her. She's got more going for her than just a pretty face. If I have anything to do with it, that face will not be pretty for much longer. You have her fingerprints. Put them through the system and see what comes up.'

"'Ella, I put her fingerprints in the system and it said 'classified.' Something is wrong. She is working for some government agency,' said Chief Wise.

"'Do you have any connections in DC that could find out who she is?' asked Ella.

"'I have one associate, but she would want to be paid a lot of money. At least $10,000 would be her asking price. If she got caught, it would mean jail time for her. Plus, I want $5,000 for my services. Everything must be in cash,' said the chief.

"'Get the information and I will pay your fees,' said Ella.

"Ella called in her circle of associates and told the situation. 'Nate and Zola, I want you to get out of the business. We are in for some hard times to come. I don't know all the details but it is not good. You are not involved in our business here in New Orleans and I want my grandchildren to grow up with a father and mother who are respected by the community for good works. So this is your last day of being involved with my enterprises,' said Ella.

"Zola was more like her mother than her father. She and Nate agreed to leave the business but both had plans to return one day," said Lola.

"Lola, Nate and Zola were your mother and father and they were truly corrupt parents," said Ted.

"Yes, now you are beginning to understand my defense," responded Lola.

"The FBI came and kept a low profile because they wanted to get the biggies at the top of the corruption ring. They started with Chief Wise. Agent Stevenson was given a team and he selected Eva to be a part of the team," said Lola.

"'Chief Wise, if you cooperate with the FBI, you will be given full immunity and will be allowed to retire with a full pension. Do you understand that this situation is serious?' said Agent Stevenson.

"Without hesitation, the chief said, 'You will have my complete cooperation.'

"The chief was a very greedy man and wanted the $5,000 that was agreed upon with Ella. That day, he went to see Ella and gave her an envelope with a detailed report on Eva. Even the changing of her name and her family history was included," said Lola.

"Chief Wise understood Ella's mentality and as he entered into the club, he pulled out his gun. 'Ella, here is the information you wanted. Now give me my money,' said the chief.

"She handed the chief an envelope with the money and after he took it, he pointed his gun at Ella, saying, 'I read the report. Eva is an FBI agent. This is the end of our relationship. Don't try to contact me about anything. I will be testifying for the FBI on your massive organization. You can expect to go to jail for life. I suggest that you leave the States today or be arrested tomorrow. They have all the proof necessary to lock you up. Eva kept a diary and has her father's detailed records.

I was told this by a close associate. Leave now before it is too late,' said Chief Wise.

"Ella sat quietly by herself and then started talking out loud, 'I will not die in jail. I will die on my own terms. First I need to tell Zola where all my money is located. The Feds will take all the nightclubs and houses but they will not get my cash.

"'Next, I will send the information to Zola in the mail and after that, I will write my own obituary. In my obituary, I will give honor to my mother, who was black, and my father, who was French. My father and mother loved each other until they died. Eddie and I loved our families and helped them when they needed it,' said Ella as she outlined her course of action out loud.

"'After I finish my paperwork, I will call my hairdresser. I want my hair, my makeup, fingernails, and toenails to look fantastic. I will put on my dress for the wake. Without telling anyone anything, after dinner I will have my favorite cup of tea and lace it with arsenic. I will lie in my bed and look like a porcelain doll baby when they find me,' thought Ella.

"Her hair was done, nails painted, makeup perfect, and after eating her favorite meal, she had her tea. That was the end of Eddie and Ella. My mother and father were standing by to take over," said Lola.

"Did anyone go to jail?" asked Ted.

"Oh yes, the FBI took the corruption case out of state. The next day, Ella's body was found by the maid. The next day, a large group of FBI agents dissented on New Orleans and broke down into small groups. The FBI was determined to send a message that the days of deep-rooted corruption was over.

"Every crook that was listed in Eva's notes and her father's records were rounded up. There so many that they had to take them to a special location for arraignment. Based on who they were, some were given limited immunity. This corruption case lasted for about five years. The FBI had a hundred percent conviction rate," said Lola.

"Eva became friends with Mr. Stevenson and one night at dinner, he said, 'My family has a strange past too. As of tonight, I want you to call me Eric. My father divorced my mother, when I was four years old, for another woman that he was in love with. I was born in Harrisonville, NC, and they lived in Harrisonville. After the divorce, my mother moved to New Orleans for a new start. As a kid growing up, my father never visited me or my mother. He would send child support on time and on my birthday and Christmas, a card with a large sum of money enclosed.

"'My mother changed my last name and her last name back to her maiden name.

"'The return address for my father was a town in California. In fact, he owned a large vineyard in southern California. My father and his wife were multi-millionaires. I went to visit them but never told my mother. I stopped in to visit their winery and taste their wines. His wife's name was Candee and his name was Frank. Located on the vineyard was a large bed and breakfast. I spent two nights there and Candee and Frank paid a lot of attention to me, but I could not bring myself to tell them who I was,' said Eric.

"'They were living in California for a reason and I didn't want to cause them harm by bringing back their past. In those few days, we became good friends and I promised to stay in touch with them. That was the last time I saw them. My cards and money continued to come. My father paid my tuition fee for all my schooling, even law school. I was hoping that he would come to my graduation ceremonies but that did not happen. While at the vineyard, I took plenty of pictures. One strange thing that struck me was that they never talked about their family. Therefore, I didn't talk about my family either,' said Eric.

"'Yesterday, I got a telegram from my father's lawyer to call him right away. There was a family emergency. I called and he gave me the bad news. Candee and my father were both killed in a car accident by a drunk driver. I needed to come to California as soon as possible. I will be leaving in the morning and will be there until I settle my father's affairs,' said Eric.

"'Would you like for me to go with you, Eric?' asked Eva.

"'No, this something I need to do on my own,' said Eric.

"Now that the New Orleans corruption cases were over, my mother and father were kept busy raising my brother and me. We were cute kids and my Uncle Nick gave my brother a nickname. His nickname was Toto. How he came up with that name always puzzled me. My brother's real name was Kevin. His nickname stuck with him and everyone called him Toto," said Lola.

"We lived just outside of New Orleans in a big white house located on thirty-five acres. The house was huge with seven bedrooms, five bathrooms, a large living room, a large kitchen, a breakfast room, a formal dining room, and a large wraparound porch. The basement had three levels. My father called it a split-level basement. The backyard had a swimming pool, a playground, a picnic grove, a bar, and a large pavilion for barbeque. My father loved his old country club in Harrisonville. It was missed by my mother and father. Because he wanted to be back in the business in some fashion, he turned the backyard into a country club. He named it Harrisonville Country Club," said Lola.

"Every Friday, Saturday, and Sunday afternoon, our country club was jumping. All the neighbors that wanted to party came to our home. My mother and her cousins would cook all day on Thursday for the weekend. At our home, we had a farm with all kinds of animals. If they were cooking chickens, she would go get a half dozen of chickens and kill them. Her cousins would help her prepare the chickens and all the side dishes and desserts. It was wonderful to see my parents enjoying themselves," said Lola.

"From Friday to Sunday, guests at the club were white and black. Spook Jackson, who lived on the farm next door, was a regular. He could play the piano by ear. Toto would sit with him and watch him play and sing. My mother was also good at playing by ear and singing. I guess I was a chip off the old block because I also had my mother's talents," said Lola.

"My father loved to drink, mostly beer, but he also made moonshine that was the favorite drink. The guests did not have to buy any food but were expected to bring Papa some beer. If beer ran out, the guests understood that they needed go get some more.

"My mother's cousin opened up a bar with a restaurant in town. He asked my mother to work for him. She worked only on Sunday nights, singing her favorite songs. The patrons loved her. Toto was very talented and Mom would take Toto with her. He could dance, sing, and play the piano and it got the crowd going. He was only about seven years old but was cute as a button. She made him a tux of all white silk with a black bowtie, white top hat, and white patent leather shoes. He was cool. His stage was the countertop of the bar," said Lola.

"What ever happened to Eric, Lola?" asked Ted.

"Eric flew out the next day to California and went straight to the vineyard. To his surprise, there was another relative that greeted him at the door. He said, 'You must be Eric, my older brother.'

"'I am Eric, but who did you say you were?' responded Eric.

"'Your brother,' replied the man.

"'My name is Robert,' said his brother.

"'I just found out about you today. They kept you a secret,' replied Robert.

"'They kept both of us a secret,' said Eric.

"'Our parents' law firm is going to read the will and a letter addressed to both of us,' said Robert.

"'May I have everyone's attention? The order of business today is to read a letter in private to Wright's two sons. After that, the will can be read,' said the executor. 'But before I get started, I'd like to say a few words about my true friends, Frank and Candee,' said the executor.

"'I was the first person that they met when they landed in California some thirty years ago. I helped them with the purchasing of the vineyard. They employed many workers and gave them fair wages. On birthdays and holidays, all employees were given bonuses. They were active members of our church. I know they had a past but we have a forgiving savior in Jesus Christ. Frank and Candee were born-again Christians. They were loved by all that knew them. Thank you,' said the executor.

"'I want to tell you two that your parents were my best friends. I don't know what is in this letter. Therefore, I am going to leave the room while you two read the letter together. This letter is for you only. What you read in the letter must stay in this room. That is what your parents wanted. They needed to tell you something so that you didn't make the same mistakes that they made. Candee told me that she didn't want that life for you two. So, read the letter and let me know when you are done,' said the executor.

"Eric said, 'After this is over, let's go somewhere so we can talk.'

"'That's okay with me,' responded Robert. 'My brother, call me Bobby,' he said.

"Eric was given the letter and he started reading.

"'To my two sons, we are very proud of the two of you. We have followed both careers. Eric is a respected lawyer with his own firm. Bobby is a federal prosecutor in the State of Louisiana. He has successfully prosecuted many cases and won. He has never lost a case.

"'Candee and I have a past that we are not proud of. We were criminals as young adults. We had a few options but we chose the worst ones. We became very wealthy off of other people's misery. Over the past thirty years, we have lived everyday trying to make others' lives better. We believe God has forgiven us. May God bless both of you!

"'We pray that the two of you become best friends. We know we robbed the two of you of many years of joy you could have experienced together. Because of our horrible past, we did not want your life affected by our sins. Now that we have crossed over, it is time for the two of you to form a bond that will allow you to grow spiritually and mentally.

"'Don't go back and try to reconstruct our past. It will only depress you. Take your inheritance and move forward. Your inheritance is all honest money. We gave away the bad money years ago, to the church and the poor. "'We have loved both of you always, your mom and dad.'

"'What do you think, Eric?' asked Bobby.

"'My emotions are mixed. I have always loved him, even at a distance. You were fortunate to have a mother and a father all your life. My mother was a good mother, so I am blessed with those memories. I did come to California and looked them up. I stayed at their bed and breakfast. They were so nice to me that I did not have the heart to tell them who I was. I was supposed to stay in touch but I felt that there was a reason for their absence from my life. I realized it was not me but them. I also went to Harrisonville and asked around about them. Many of the old-timers remembered them and told me some wild stories. I checked some of the court records but there was not much available. Based on the interviews with the older residents, our parents were gangsters. I would just like to let it go. What happened in Harrisonville should die in Harrisonville,' said Eric.

"'I agree and I would like for you to know that they knew who you were. I found a picture years ago of you at your high school graduation. He kept it in his Bible. I asked my mother who the boy was in the picture and she said: someone that you will love and get to know some day,' said Bobby.

"'I believe they decided years ago that their past was not going to interfere with our lives. They left all their best friends behind and never looked back or returned,' said Eric.

"At the reading of the will, the executor stared at it. It was amazing how much wealth they had accumulated throughout the years. 'The Wrights left $5,000.00 per person to everyone who is currently working for them. A college fund will be set up for migrant workers' children to go to college. The church will receive ten percent of their total assets. The administrative staff is to receive $100,000 each. The balance will be divided between our two sons, Eric and Robert. Please use your gifts wisely to make better your lives and that of others. That is what your parents wanted for you,' said the executor. "'In conclusion, Frank and Candee want to be cremated and don't want to have any type of memorial. They want their ashes to be sprinkled around the graves of their best friends from Harrisonville. They are Buddy Miller, Redd Harrison, and Nina Harrison. I believe they are all in the same graveyard,' said the executor.

"'If it is okay with you, we can work and do everything together,' said Eric.

"'That sounds like a good plan,' responded Bobby.

"'Let's write out a plan of what we need to do. Since we are both lawyers, we can do all our legal work. The plan should include selling all of their assets and then dividing them up between us. We should give out all the money gifts to their staff and workers as soon as possible,' said Eric.

"Bobby looked at Eric and said, 'I believe they are the last of their generation including their close friends. Maybe we should have the minister come to the house and say a prayer for blessing them and their friends,' said Bobby.

"Eric looked like he wanted to cry. His sadness spilled over into Bobby and they both sat down and the tears rolled down their weary faces. 'Let's go and get something to eat. We need to keep up our strength and health because we have a tough job ahead of us,' said Bobby.

"As they were cleaning out their parents' papers, Eric found a file box that was locked. 'I wonder what's in this box. If it is locked, then it must be important,' said Eric.

"It took a lot of effort to get the box opened; it had Bobby's birth certificate. Bobby kept staring at the paper and then he dropped it on the floor, stating, 'My whole life has been a lie. Oh my, what a lie! They should have told me. I would have understood.'

"Eric picked up the paper and realized that Buddy Miller was Bobby's biological father and Frank had adopted him at birth. 'Bobby, get over it. What difference does it make that you didn't come from Frank's bloodline? You were loved and received the best education possible. You are the attorney general for the State of Louisiana. When we are born, we have no say as to who will nurture and raise us. It is God's will as to what path He set for us to follow. They might not have been scumbags in their early lives but became better people after God showed them the way. Forgive them, the same way I did many years ago,' said Eric.

"'You are right. Let's move on to Harrisonville to spread their ashes,' said Bobby.

"Eva and Nick were seeing each other often and had fallen in love. My father wanted to know more about his family's history. He felt that if they had children, it would be important to understand and know your family. He knew the best place to start was Harrisonville," said Lola.

"'Do you want me to go to Harrisonville with you?' asked Eva.

"'Yes, I just want closure on that generation. They were a group of friends that functioned like a family of criminals. I'd like to see their graves and say a prayer for their souls. Maybe my brother and Zola will go with us,' said Nick.

"Nate and Zola did not really want to go back to Harrisonville but he knew it would make his brother happy. Within a few weeks, they were off to Harrisonville. Even though my brother and I were babies, they took us with them," said Lola.

"As they approached the gravesite, they saw Mr. Stevenson from New Orleans standing in front of my grandparents' headstones. Beside him was another man that Nick recognized as the state attorney general for the State of Louisiana.

"'Oh my,' said Nick, 'our past will not let go of us. I hope they are not trying to pin anything on us. Please God, let it be for something good and not bad,' he begged silently to himself with his head bowed.

"'Hello Eric, your telegram said for you to come to California but here you are in Harrisonville. I know you were born in Harrisonville, but why are you standing over Nick and Nate's parents' graves?' asked Eva.

"'You are right; I did go to California. I will be going back in the morning. This is my brother Bobby. We are following our parents' wishes to sprinkle their ashes over their best friends' graves. They are Buddy Miller, Redd, and Nina Harrison,' said Eric.

"Nate just stood there and suddenly took a few steps back. 'Your parents knew them?' asked Nate.

"Bobby spoke up, 'They were their best friends and partners here in Harrisonville.'

"'Wow! We came here for closure on that generation and met up by fate with decedents of the same generation,' said Nick.

"'Let's spread the ashes and say a prayer. Maybe your family will join us for a bite to eat. This way, we can help each other to find closure,' said Eric.

"'God, forgive them for all their sins, amen!' said Nick.

"'After today, this will be my last time I will meet with your families on a social or professional level. As you know, I am the state attorney for the State of Louisiana. In the future, we might meet again but it will not be social,' said Bobby.

"'You Harrison boys were born and raised in Harrisonville. Tell us how it was growing up with these two families of friends. Don't hold back anything. I want to hear

95

the good and the bad, okay?' He was looking very serious as he ordered his lunch.

"'As kids, we observed many of their activities. One thing good about our conversation is that they are dead and their crimes will go to the grave with them. I would like for you, Bobby, to give Nate and me full immunity from any legal actions for information given to you about this family of organized gangsters. Full immunity at all levels, criminal or civil actions,' said Nick.

"'We want protection for all our assets. Even though they were criminals, we have lived an honest adult life. We should not have to pay for their crimes,' said Nate.

"'If you write out a contract giving us full immunity and all the items I have mentioned, we can all sign it and tonight in your hotel room, I will give you all the information that will enable you to find answers to closed cases,' said Nick.

"That night, they met Bobby in his hotel room. The contract was reviewed by Nate and Nick. After a few more negotiations on different issues, the immunity was agreed upon and signed on the letterhead," said Lola.

"'Nina, Candee, Redd, Buddy, and Frank were all friends whose friendship was sealed with a long history of crime that started as young kids. They were a group of criminals who functioned like a family,' said Nick

"'Before you get started, I want you to know that this is being recorded, understood?' said Eric.

"'Yes, we understand,' responded Nate.

"'To begin with, this family of criminals was just kids when they started their career as gangsters. What we are about to tell you was witnessed by us, Nate and Nick Harrison. Other accounts were told to us by one of them, or overheard, or we took part in the criminal act,' said Nick.

"'Redd, our father, came here with our grandparents from Ireland. They were forced to leave because of being bootleggers and were about to go to jail. They had money and purchased a farm. They raised corn for consumption, animals, and moonshine. Business was going very well. His brother-in-law, who was a drunk, came to our home to rob my grandfather late one night after my grandmother had passed away. In the process, he woke up and was killed by his brother-in-law. Redd grabbed his handgun, which he called Sue, and shot him. That was the first person he killed at the age of sixteen. The local police liked the Harrison family and just wrote it off as self-defense. When we were about twenty-two years old, just out of college, our father executed a bootlegger competitor named Jumbo. He shot him up close in the head. We both witnessed this event. They had a gambling hall, prostitution business in which most of the town's big shots patronized often. I know this for a fact because we were regular non-paying customers,' said Nick.

"'Our mother, Nina, ran the prostitution business. She called it the Gentlemen's Basement. Most of the women were flown into Harrisonville from foreign countries for the purpose of prostitution. Their biggest reward was living in the States. Nina was extremely beautiful and was very sweet. She was loved by all that met her. She would never hurt anyone. Even if someone could not pay their bill in full at the end of the month, she would let them slide,' said Nate.

"'One day, I was looking through some papers and saw plans and blueprints for a resort in the Bahamas. I asked my father about the plans and he said, 'Do unto others before they do unto you. I had a partner in the Bahamas named Lyle and he stole from me a lot of money. Later, I found out he was the mayor's baby brother and a crook. He refused to refund my money, so I killed him and left the Bahamas. That was the end of my Bahamas dream.'

"'I am not sure how many people my father killed but there are many buried in the farm's swamp. Candee was also very good-looking. She was everything you could ask for in a lady. She had a secret personality. People that worked for her or knew her well nicknamed her the smiling assassin. She ran the bank. It was used for loansharking. If a client owed a large sum and was far behind in their payments, she would have Frank to have an insurance policy taken out on that person and after about six months or more, she would have the client killed and would collect on the policy. All the members of this family group of criminals were horrifying but she was the worst,' said Nate.

"'Buddy and Redd were teenagers when they teamed up to pursue their careers as criminals together. Based on the stories they told us, they were instant friends and were born to be criminals. Their motto was: friends to the end. Sure enough that was how they ended their lives as criminals who were friends to the end,' said Nick.

"'Buddy was the CEO of business. He kept abreast of all the income money and all the payouts. He conducted weekly meetings in order to determine if changes needed to take place. He determined whether or not to purchase real estate or how to get it for free. He loved the word 'free.' Buddy would go to the tax sales in the county and buy up tax liens. He was not liked by some of Harrison County's residents because of his overreaching of tax liens. If a resident approached him with anger about his buying of liens, he would say, 'Pay your taxes or your home will be my home.' He turned the homes into rental properties and the businesses. He would build them up and when he was legally able, he would sell the business for a profit,' said Nick.

"'Buddy was not a killer; that was Redd's department. Buddy was all business and money. Buddy would have you beaten up by one of his goons. If you didn't come around to his way of thinking, he would inform Redd and the situation would be solved. Buddy was killed by an associate and Redd took over everything. He was doing a good job but hung out every night till very late. Redd was murdered by Rita, our stepmother. We took everything of value out of the house and, with the sheriff's blessings, we burned the house down with the two dead bodies inside. One thing we discovered was Buddy's journal. It had a log of all the income money and payout that took place daily. That senator, who was indicted on federal charges that was given total immunity to testify against Redd's indictment on many charges, was poisoned by Frank on Candee's orders. They used rat poison, which is hard to detect,' said Nate.

"'The journal listed all the important people that were on the payroll. Some names had a line drawn through them. That signified that these people were eliminated. The senator's name was in the book, with a line through his name. I have the book but would like to keep it for a while. It is like an insurance policy in many ways,' said Nick.

"'Oh my,' said Bobby, 'our parents were awful people. While growing up, they hid their past well from me, as if it was hard for them to even kill an insect. They loved both of us boys and did not want anything to interfere in our lives as honest adults. They did a good job. I feel that was their small way of easing the pain of the past. On holidays, I would hear my mother crying and my father talking to her. He would hold her for hours while they played religious hymns. They never got over the past but continued to live the best they knew how. I believe that is what's next for all of us,' said Bobby.

"'Here is the tape; this family group of criminals is gone. Their sins died with them. Keep the tape and keep it safe. You never know when it might come in handy. I often tell young people; you know where you've been but you don't know where you are going. It was nice meeting you two guys, and maybe in the future we will meet up again on a happier occasion,' said Bobby."

"Lola, did they ever get together again?" asked Ted.

"No, Bobby resigned from the position of state attorney general and married his childhood sweetheart. My father received a postcard from him years ago, sent from Paris, France. That was the end of their relationship. Because of his family history, it was believed that he felt he was the wrong person for that position.

"Nick built a beautiful boathouse on the river here in New Orleans. He now works for legal aid, helping poor people get justice. I understand he works for free. Last year, there was a big write-up in the local paper about his success stories. He has also sponsored a full four-year scholarship to one student with outstanding grade and good citizenship. He is around but does not get involved with our family," said Lola.

"My mother Zola loved working for her cousin and my father loved his country club. My mother was only nineteen when she married my father and he was twenty-six. The age difference didn't matter at first, but after we were born, she wanted more than just being a Sunday-afternoon singer. She did not want any more children. She would tell her family and friends that two were enough.

"Zola did get pregnant and I had the cutest little baby sister, her name Janet. She looked like an angel. In fact, Mom called her Angel. Toto and I were three years old when Janet was born, and Mom was spending more and more time at her cousin's restaurant and bar. She was not just working. She was having fun with the customers, especially the men," said Lola.

"During the week, Mom would go out partying with her girlfriends. Pop opened up a liquor store down by harbor. He worked for long hours even after the store had closed. Sometimes he would get home after two o'clock in the morning. He didn't need the money but just wanted to be in the loop. He wanted to work and be an honest husband and father.

"Mom, on the other hand, felt that Papa was getting too old for her and she started meeting up with guys of her age. She would invite them to Papa's country club. They would come with beer and eat and drink all evening and into the early morning," said Lola.

"Some of Mom's girlfriends were very outgoing and would flirt with Papa. 'Keep your fucking hands off my man. I have had three babies for him and he belongs to me,' Mom would shout.

"The girlfriends would back off but Papa would get drunk and pursue them, stating, 'You look so good. You look like angels from heaven.' He spoke like a player.

"Mom walked up to Papa and cracked him in the head with anything she could find. Sometimes it would be a bottle, dinner plate, or whatever," said Lola.

"Papa was trying very hard to be an honest man. His country club on the weekends was his way of filling in that desire for criminal activity. Mom, on the other hand, didn't give a damn. She missed her parents and her enjoyment of singing every night. One night, Mom slipped out on Papa while he was at his liquor store, working late. She left us with a teenager. Mom had turned on the iron to press a dress. She went out of Harrison County to get an abortion. She forgot to turn the iron off and the house went up in flames," said Lola.

"Karen, the babysitter, got my brother and me out but forgot about Janet until she turned around looking at the burning house. Yelling at the top of her voice, she yelled, 'There is one more!'

"By that time, it was too late to try to save Janet. Janet was only three years old and had a very short life," said Lola with her eyes tearing.

"'Do you know where Mrs. Harrison is, Karen?' asked the fire marshal.

"'Not exactly, she said she was going to visit a friend in the next county. She left a phone number. She told me she would be home very late,' said Karen.

"Papa was called and was told to come home now, for there was a family emergency. As he drove up, he could smell smoke and see the flames. 'Oh no, not my home, not my family. God, please save them and keep them safe!' he said to himself as the fire chief stopped him from going too close.

"'What about my family? Are my kids and wife safe?' he asked.

"'Nate, do you know where your wife is?' asked the chief.

"'She is supposed to be home with the kids,' responded Nate.

"'Well, she isn't,' said the chief.

"The whole yard was full with family, neighbors, and onlookers. My cousin Amy came up to my father and said, 'Come with me, Nate. We need to talk to you.'

"'Where are the kids?' asked Nate.

"'They took them to the hospital to check them out,' she responded.

"The fire was out and only the smell of smoke and burned wood filled the night air. My sister was the cutest little girl who was full of joy and life," said Lola as tears flowed down her lovely cheeks.

"Nate screamed at the top of his lungs over and over again, stating, 'My God! Why Janet?' Finally he remembered he had two other children and a wife. 'Where is the rest of my family?' asked Nate.

"The chief responded, 'We took the children to the hospital just for a routine check-up. Janet is also there.'

"'Where is my wife?' asked Nate.

"'We were hoping you could tell us,' responded the chief.

"'She was home when I left to go to my store. She did not have any plan to go out tonight that she shared with me,' said Nate.

"'The babysitter told us that she only said she would be home late,' said the chief.

"The sun was rising as Zola was almost home. The air was full of strange smells. The smell of death was the most obvious smell which was mixed with a strong, smoky, nose-burning odor. Zola started coughing as she approached her home.

"'Oh, oh, what happened to my home? Where are my children?' asked Zola. As she got out of her red Cadillac, her cousin approached.

"'There has been a terrible tragedy. Come home with me and I will explain everything to you,' said the cousin.

"Her cousin Barbara fixed her a cup of tea. 'First of all, the children are at the hospital for a check-up. They are okay. Nate is there with them. You look awful, Zola. You take one of my sleeping pills and Nate will talk to you later,' said Barbara.

"Barbara called the hospital to speak to Nate and told him that Zola was at her home sleeping and she didn't know anything about Janet. 'That is your job to tell her,' said Barbara.

"Sometime in the late evening, Zola woke up and my brother and I were sitting on the bed. Nate was sitting in the chair. The doctor had given him a sedative, for he was about to go out of his mind," said Lola.

"'Where is Janet?' asked Zola.

Toto, with a loving voice, responded, 'With God.'

"Zola looked at my father and us children and started yelling, 'No! No! No! Not my baby!'

"My mother's crying was out of control, so they sent us in the next room to be with Cousin Barbara," said Lola.

"'Zola, you know I love you. We will get through these hard days so that we can live on and enjoy our children. But I need you to tell me the truth. I might not forgive you today but I will in the future,' said Nate.

"'Nate, I went out of the county to get an abortion. I didn't want any more children. Three are enough. I left them with a reliable babysitter. I don't understand why our home caught fire and burned down,' said Zola.

"Zola saw Nate's face turn beet-red and he looked like fire was coming out of his head. At this moment, he was his father's son. He even looked like Redd. Zola realized that nothing would ever be the same.

"Zola fell back into the bed, thinking to herself, 'I have lost Janet and now I have lost Nate. What is left for me in this world? My parents are gone and now my family.'

"With tears dropping from his chin, Nate stood up over Zola, stating the following, 'I have loved you from the day I saw you. I have watched you coming and going out with single girlfriends. As long as you came home to me at night, it was okay. But this is unacceptable. As of this moment, we will be husband and wife but nothing will ever be the same. One last thing, was this my baby?'

"With her eyes closed, Zola responded, 'Yes.'

"Nick moved Nate and his family into his boathouse on the river. He understood the whole situation from all sides. He felt that the calming waves of the water would help Zola recover from her sorrows faster. A nurse was hired to take care of her because she had a nervous breakdown after finding out that the cause of the fire was her fault. According to the fire chief, the iron was left on, sitting flat down on the board," said Lola.

"After a few months, Mom got up from her bed and said to the nurse that she was no longer needed. 'I will take care of my husband and children.'

"My father had a new home rebuilt right on the same spot of the original home. We continued to live with my Uncle Nick until the new home was ready. He made us enjoy living with him.

"Uncle Nick was always the most honest of all my relatives. He worked hard while in law school and graduated. He was number one in his class. He was also president of his senior undergraduate class at Harvard. As a small child, I wanted to be honest and a good civic-minded resident of Louisiana. But that never happened. Our home was rebuilt and we moved back home to Vinton," said Lola.

"My father allowed my mother's cousins to run the liquor store while my mother and father hung out at the racetrack. They were at home at the track and appeared to have forgotten about Janet. This racetrack had secret areas inside that were known only to special people. My mother and father were considered special people. Mom was a good flirt, so she decided to ask their friend about the owner if she could open up a gentlemen's room for very special clients," said Lola.

"'If you allow me to run the room, it will enhance your other activities such as your secret poker room and the after hour's liquor sales. I have lots of experience because I was in charge of this business in Harrisonville for many years. In Harrisonville, it was called the Gentlemen's Basement,' said Zola.

"Without much thought, Lenny, the owner, said, 'Sounds good to me. I will set up the business but after it is making a profit, you will have to pay all the expenses and give me sixty-five percent of all profit from all sources. This will be your business and your responsibility for activities, legal and questionable.'

"'It will not take me long to start making a profit. We have friends in New Orleans that will deliver the liquor well below wholesale prices. My husband and I will bring in our associates from Harrisonville and New Orleans who are the top professional in this line of business,' said Zola.

"The racetrack became a full service operation. Live racing, poker room, after-hours speakeasy, and prostitutes for clients that wanted to have a good time were provided by Nate and Zola.

"The racetrack owner was known to be a crook. During a big purse race, the management would fix the race so that a 75 to 1 horse would win over much better horses. This way, the owner and his friends would have a big payday," said Lola.

"Lola, next week I will be receiving from the prosecutor's office all his discovery information. He will want our information too. But I have to be careful not to give away our defense. I believe we are halfway home. Because of personal reasons, I will be stepping down as your attorney after we finish with your story. I will be assisting the new attorney. I have talked it over with my boss and he feels that I should step down. You will not be going to jail. I guarantee the verdict will be one that will be in your favor," said Ted.

Lola looked at Ted and for the first time she could see love in his eyes. 'Who is this Ted?' Lola thought to herself. 'He is my lawyer. He is tall and handsome. Maybe I should interview him. No, I will wait until the trial is over. He might think I am trying to hit on him. We have a good relationship and I do not want to destroy it by acting like a classless bitch,' Lola thought to herself.

"Okay, Lola, tell me about the business, and did anything spectacular happen to them while working at the track?" asked Ted.

"Yes, my mother kept getting pregnant every twelve months," said Lola.

"Well, I thought the twins were her only children," responded Ted.

"We are her only living children. She ended up having six full-term babies. After delivery, they would live a few hours or for a few days and die before coming home. Her first dead baby had a big knock on his head. It was a boy and she named him Henry. She said she hit herself on the end of a table at the track. But I witnessed her and my father fighting. She hit him in the head with a tire iron and was running away from him and tripped.

"This took place at home and an ambulance was called and the police came too. Mama told them that he was drunk and fell down the steps. Papa seconded the lie.

"She always started the arguments. Most of the time it was because she would overhear Papa making a pass at a woman. His favorite line was: 'You look so good, and in fact you look like an angel that just fell from heaven.' That was all she needed to hear and she would get off on him. Fire would be coming from her eyes. Her favorite statement was: 'I have had babies for you and you son-of-a-bitch trying to give everything away to another woman. You old fart.'

"The next baby had an enlarged heart, mainly because of Mama's poor diet which included drinking and smoking. This baby lasted a full day. It was a boy and he was named James. The next baby, she was a girl, her name Susan, and Mama had to have a Cesarean Section because the cord was wrapped around the baby's neck. The baby died and Mama was depressed for a long time but she continued to work at the track.

"She appeared to get pregnant every twelve months. Papa would question whether he was the father. That would set her off. She would start drinking and when she was nasty drunk, she would just go right up to him with whatever was in her hands and start hitting him. Papa would never fight back. But he did try to protect himself. Every time she would hit him, it was on his head. She would call the ambulance and tell the police some made-up story and he would go along with it.

"It was about two years before she had the forth baby. This baby was born with a skin over its face and suffocated. It was a boy and only lived a few minutes after birth. His name was John. The fifth baby was a girl and she was turned upside down and Mama had to have a second Cesarean Section. She died the next day because her weak heart could not handle the trauma.

"The last baby was born dead. It was a boy, and she named him Enough Harrison. Mama had gained a little weight but still had sex appeal. I was about eleven years old and stayed home from school because I was sick. Papa was at the track and Mama stayed home with me. I was in the bed and one of Papa's friends from the track stopped by. His name was John. He was my father's best friend. I could hear them talking in the kitchen but they did not see or hear me. As I was listening, it was obvious that they were lovers. Mama was trying to figure out how to get rid of Papa," said Lola.

"John looked at her and said, 'Just hit him in the head with a baseball bat and tell the cops it was self-defense.'

"Mama said, 'Oh no, I could never kill him. He is the father of my children. He has loved me even with all my bad habits. We have been through a lot of ups and downs. I will just divorce him.'

"So that was the plan. As John was driving home, his breaks on his truck froze as he was trying to turn the corner leading up to his street. His truck struck a pole and he was killed instantly. He died that day and so did Mama's heart," said Lola.

"Instead of being depressed, she decided to get back into action with her cooking, singing, dancing, and piano-playing at the special room at the track," said Lola.

"'Nate, I am going to purchase a baby grand piano for the bar area at the track, set up a New Orleans' style restaurant, and have live music on Friday, Saturday, and Sunday afternoons. It will be called Zola's Lounge,' said Zola.

"'Maybe Toto can play the piano, sing, and dance with you on Sunday afternoons. He loves music and is very talented in many areas. Just like his mother,' said Nate.

"Toto's real name was Kevin but he was given this nickname by my mother because he loved dancing on his toes when he heard music. Therefore, she named him Toto. Plus, she loved the name because she said it sounded like a name for a gangster. She was right. The name was perfect, and he became a gangster," said Lola.

"'As the owner of the track, Zola, I am very pleased with your innovations which will increase our numbers for the poker room and at the same time provide an extra incentive for customers to come often,' responded Hank.

"Mama worked day and night getting the restaurant set up. She ordered the piano and got local talent to play for her on the weekends. Toto was featured on Sunday afternoons. We were eleven and a half years old when we were both introduced to the world of criminal activity. Toto was in the entertainment part and I worked in the kitchen. We both were tall and looked older than our age. We loved the business. We both wanted to learn everything about running the business. At the time, we did not know it was mostly illegal," said Lola.

"Opening night came and the people were pouring in. The room held two hundred and fifty people and the line was all the way out to the racetrack area. It now cost $5.00 just to get inside. Mama did two shows per night and only one show on Sunday afternoons. People waited at the door. If someone left, then someone could come in. That is how packed it was.

"Mama would open up with Blueberry Hill and the room would go wild. After she was singing and playing, Scooby Johnson, a local, would keep them going with saxophone, jazz, in New Orleans style. Even though I was young, I helped keep the food flowing. Mama would come in the kitchen when she could to check on things. At 2:00 a.m., the Zola's Lounge was closed and the special people were allowed to stay. After 2:00 a.m., the after-hour bar would be opened alone with Gentlemen's Basement.

"Behind the bar, they sold Cuban cigars that were smuggled in from Cuba. Also, any type of dope could be purchased. Clients had an ID number. Without your number, you could not purchase any cigars or drugs," said Lola.

"Toto was featured for Sunday afternoons; he was the afternoon sensation. It cost $6.00 to get in on Sunday for the show. Toto would come out on stage in his white tux with tails. He was good-looking and had brown skin. He was tall and looked much older than he was. As soon as he walked out, the room burst into a thunder of clapping. The band would play a song that he could tap dance to and he just took off like Sammy Davis Jr. Next, he went to the piano and would hit a few notes and then start playing and singing rock-and-roll songs that the crowd in the room loved. That was Toto, the great entertainer," said Lola.

"Everything was going wonderful. Mama and Papa were getting along better and she was not beating on him anymore. Papa was a big gambler and had lost large amounts of money betting on the horse and playing poker. He did not tell Mama because she would have been furious. Therefore, he decided to go to the tax office and buy up homes that were up for tax sale. These homes would become rental homes. Good money was coming from the business. Their forty percent of the profit made them very rich. Zola did not allow Papa to handle any of this money. She knew that he had become a gambler and did not want their money to be used for gambling. She was thinking ahead for their children's future education which included college and beyond," said Lola.

"Papa took the money he had left from his inheritance and invested into real estate. He became the main buyer at the tax sales. In fact, sometimes he was the only buyer. He became the go-to person for rental homes in and around town. His waterfront properties were very popular. He turned them into condos.

"In some circles, he was a hated man. His business practices were very rough and questionable in many situations.

I was with Papa when a man came up to him and said, 'Fuck you, Nate. You took my brother's home. One day, you will get yours taken.' Papa just looked at him and said, 'I hope your taxes are paid up, because your home will be next.' I just put my head down in shame," said Lola.

"When clients received credit in order to play poker and were behind in paying off their debts, Papa would hire collectors to go get their money. I had heard stories about my grandfather, Redd, and his criminal mind and activities. It was becoming obvious that my father was more like his father than Nick. But when it came to Zola, she was as gentle as a kitty cat. Papa would tell the collectors not to come back empty-handed. 'If they want to settle out with me, I will meet with them.' In most cases, the clients knew it was either the money or their life. Papa had a solution to that problem. They would have to make him beneficiary to any insurance policy and prove that payments were being made. Or if it was a large sum of money, they were required to sign over their deed to transfer their homes to him. He did not care if the client was male or female, blind, cripple, or crazy. He wanted his money. At the end, he got paid," said Lola.

"'Nate, soon we will have enough money saved that we can send our two bright children to any university in the States. Just like you and Nick. Toto and Lola both wanted to get a degree in business and I told them not to stop there to go for their MBAs. I want them to work and earn an honest living. This life is all we know. Maybe if our parents had kept us away from this life, things might have been different, but it is what it is. We cannot go back. It is too late for us,' said Zola.

"Zola and Nate understood that paying taxes at all levels was important and they hired the best accountant to handle their business. He paid all their taxes on time and they trusted him completely. Mama decided that she wanted a bigger home by the river and did not want a mortgage. She had planned to pay with cash. They planned to rent out our old home. The home on the river was priced at $1.1 million. It was beautiful. Just close your eyes and anything you could dream of was in this home. Mama wrote a check for the deposit which was twenty percent of the selling price. After a few weeks, the bank notified them that their check bounced, and my parents were horrified," said Lola.

"'Nate, there must be a mistake. Did you spend all our money?' asked Zola.

"'No, I never touched any of it. I have enough in my saving to buy your dream home. I will call Gary, our accountant, and see what happened to the money. Gary will have the answer.'

"'Gary does not manage my money. I do it myself. Remember, I do have a degree in business,' said Nate.

"Zola was extremely upset; she had worked hard for her money by not going on big, expensive vacations. She did not want to wait for the next day. That night, she went to Gary's home to talk to him about the bad check. She knocked on the door several times real hard. No one answered and it appeared that they had left. All the furniture was gone. She turned the door handle and it opened. As she walked in, she knew he had stolen all of their money.

"The next day, Mama went to the bank and there was only $100.00 in the account. Gary had forged her signature on several checks over a three-month period until he wiped out the account. Gary skipped town with his family," said Lola.

"'Nate, we cannot let him get away with our money. We will have to hunt him down and get our money back. My parents had a private eye which was very good. I will call him and ask him to take our case. When he finds him, he will get it back or he will never live to spend it,' said Zola.

"The next day, Mama called Bruce and gave him all the details. "'Bruce, he took $1.9 million from my account. I want every penny back. If he has it in the bank, take him to the bank and get it. Return him to his home, tie up him and his wife, and burn their home down with them in it. Do not harm their children. Do it when the kids are at school. If you need to, wait until the time is right. But get the job done. Your payday will be $100,000.00. I know I can depend on you. My parents believed in you, and you are the best,' said Zola.

"That night, Mama poured herself a big glass of whisky on the rocks and sat in the family room in the dark. When Papa came home, he saw Mama sitting in the dark with her drink. At that moment, he could see her mother's personality in Zola. The fun-loving young girl he met years ago was gone. All that was left was an almost thirty-five-year-old woman who was out to get even with her thief," said Lola.

"It took about a week for Bruce to find Gary. He was so dumb. He went to New Orleans, Zola's hometown. Anything that happened to him would go unnoticed. Murder was common in New Orleans. For him, Zola should have been the last person to steal from.

"Within two weeks, Zola received a cashier's check from Bruce. He had recovered all the money. When he returned, Bruce filled her in on the details. 'He did not have a wife or children. He lived by himself. He is dead. I burned him up in his house. I made it look like an accident. He was an outsider and no one will care. But he did tell me that he was made to take the money by an old man with a Caribbean accent who appeared to be from the Bahamas or from that area. He also said that the man was going to kill him and hunt down and kill his sisters and brother if he did not steal the money,' said Bruce.

"Mama became very concerned. She told Nate the story and he knew exactly who it was. 'Zola, we might be in trouble. This old man is the brother of the conman that my father killed in the Bahamas before Nick and I were born. He must have figured it out that it was my father who killed his brother. My father is dead, so he wants revenge. I do not think he wants to physically harm us but we must find him. My father lived by his words. Do unto others before they do unto you,' said Nate.

"'Where do we start?' asked Zola.

"'I have some old papers of my father. Maybe I can get a name from them,' responded Nate.

"The next morning, Nate called Uncle Nick," said Lola.

"'Nick, I need you to come for a visit. Some very troubling situation has surfaced from the past that involves us. Please come as soon as possible,' said Nate.

"'New Orleans is only a two-hour drive to Vinton. I will leave after breakfast,' Nick said to Eva, who now was living with him.

"'I will go with you. Maybe I can help in some small way,' replied Eva.

"'I wonder what from the past could cause concerns for us today. My brother wants me to bring any pictures or papers that I might have of my parents and their friends. I have plenty of pictures and papers. The pictures were all dated and the people were named. My mother did that because she wanted her boys to understand the past so that we would have a good life without criminal activities. My parents were born criminals. A psychologist would tell that criminals are not born but are made. Sorry, that is not the case with my parents. My grandparents were criminals, my parents were criminals, and my brother is a criminal. I pray to God that my nephew and niece grow up to be good citizens,' said Nick.

"The next morning, Nick and Eva arrived with boxes and papers, some of the papers no one had ever looked at until now. We were asked to go into the family room while the adults sat and had coffee in the kitchen with the boxes. We could hear everything. As we listened, it became known to us that our family has a dark, sinister past," said Lola.

"'What is this?' asked Eva as she held up a small blue notebook that was covered with mold and pages that were sticking together. 'I think this is your father's confession book.' Eva took a thin knife and carefully separated the pages. She began to read the first page.

"'I have kept a record of all my criminal activity. One day, after my generation is long gone, the authorities will be able to solve murders and other crimes that have gone unsolved for many years. This is my way of asking God to forgive me for taking this path in life,' submitted Redd Harrison.

"'The date and time of the murder is recorded and the circumstance that led up to the murder. This book needs to be turned over to the FBI,' said Eva.

"'That might be true, but for now we need to find the name of this old man who wants to harm us. I believe his name is here somewhere, okay,' said Nick.

"'Redd's first murder was his uncle who killed his father while trying to rob him. His second murder was a competitor who beat him up and killed some of his workers. The next was his cousin, for his land and insurance money. The last was Lyle from the Bahamas who was the mayor's baby brother. This is it, jackpot. His name is Lyle. All we have to do is find out the name of the mayor during that time. After that, we can develop a plan to stop this man who is trying to get revenge after all these years,' said Eva.

"The next day, I was looking at the pictures of my grandparents. They were good-looking people. Their friends were also good-looking. In order to make a living in their line of business, they were very smart people. It is a shame that it was not developed differently like the Rockefellers," said Lola.

"As the adults sat in kitchen looking through papers, Nick said, 'Let's hire Bruce to find him but he is not to approach him. Just let us know where he is. Bruce can find a needle in a haystack.'

"'That sounds good but you are not going to harm him. If you do, you will be just like your parents,' said Eva.

"'Let's have a drink,' said Zola.

"No one said anything, so Zola poured herself a big glass of wine.

"'We need a plan. After he finds the old man and then what and who will go to talk to him without being aggressive,' said Nick.

""All eyes turned to Nick; he was the lawyer and could give the old man some legal reasons to leave the children of Redd alone.

"Without hesitating, Nick said, 'Okay.'

"Bruce was hired and was told only to report back to Nick the old man's location. It took Bruce longer than normal to find the man but he did. Bruce had gotten a picture from the Bahamas of their former mayor. The man was staying in New Orleans and was spotted at the bank talking to the bank manager about the money the accountant had deposited in the bank a few months ago. The old man did not know that the accountant was dead. All he knew was that the money had been deposited into the bank with both of their names on the account.

"'The account was closed out a few months ago and all the money was withdrawn?' asked the old man.

"Hearing that news, the old man knew that this family of criminals was on to him and that he would be lucky to get away with his life. Bruce followed the man back to his hotel and called Nick.

"'Nick, the old man is staying at The Fish Bone Hotel of New Orleans. I am in the lobby. Do you want me to stay here until you get to the hotel?' asked Bruce.

"'Yes, I will come now. How did you find him?' asked Nick.

"'He was at the bank, trying to withdraw the money and found out it was gone,' responded Bruce.

"'Oh, Nick, he is in the lobby with his suitcase. It looks like he is getting out of town,' said Bruce.

"'Follow him. Do not let him out of your sight,' responded Nick.

"The old man went to the airport where he had a ticket for going back to the Bahamas, and Bruce called Nick. 'He is on his way home. The Harrisons name must have scared him, especially since all the money was gone. Maybe he figured he should get out now before he loses not only the money but also his life,' said Bruce.

"Nick was happy to hear the news but he did not know that Bruce had murdered the accountant. He did know that murder was part of his duties when he worked for Zola's parents," said Lola.

"'Thank goodness that's over. Maybe now we can plan our wedding,' said Eva.

"Nate knew something was wrong with Zola but could not figure it out. She was drinking very heavily and working longs hours at the track. My father did not want her to have any more pregnancies, so he went and got fixed. He did not tell Zola. He thought it would upset her.

"My father made sure that she got her dream home. He was hoping this would bring her back to the woman he knew, who loved life and was happy to be alive. The new home did nothing for my mother.

"Nick always wanted to have a wife and children, and now he had the perfect woman who wanted to be called Mrs. Nicholas Young Harrison. He had waited a long time for Eva. Eva no longer worked for the FBI. With money not being an issue, she planned the wedding with very little help from a wedding planner.

"It was a beautiful spring night as Eva and Nick sat on the deck of his boathouse making plans for the future. She put her head on his shoulder and closed her eyes. He leaned over and kissed her forehead. 'Nothing will ever come between us; our marriage will be blessed by God. I would like to get married in a church,' said Nick.

"'Oh, I was hoping that we would get married in my church. I pay my ties every month. My mother will be looking down on us with her blessings. God knows your goodness and so do I,' said Eva.

"Just then, there was a loud knocking at the front door. It was Zola. 'Can I stay with you because Nate might kill me?!' yelled Zola.

"'What's going on?' asked Eva.

"'I am pregnant,' she responded.

"'That is wonderful,' responded Nick and Eva.

"'No, it's not!' said Zola, yelling and screaming like a wild woman.

"'Tonight I told Nate I was pregnant and he flipped out and was calling me all kinds of names. He said I was a fucking bitch. He said I was just like my mother and maybe I should do all of us a favor and commit suicide like my mother. I ran out of the house and came straight here,' said Zola.

"'I don't understand. Why was he so upset to that point?' asked Nick.

"'He had himself fixed about a year ago and did not tell me. This baby is not his,' said Zola.

"'Oh no, I think it is time for a drink,' said Nick.

"'A drink, I need more than a drink. I need an abortion,' said Zola.

"'Come with me and I am going to run the water so that you can take a hot bath. We will figure all of this out tomorrow,' said Eva.

"The next morning, Zola got up early and appeared to be ready to leave. 'Good morning, family. I had a good night's sleep, the best I have had in years. I thought about my past and what I need to do for my future. The first thing is to look at the truth. I will never be happy if I do not accept the truth about my parents and how I have been living my life,' said Zola.

"'My parents lived a life as professional criminals. They loved me but provided their type of lifestyle for me. To begin with, my grandmother was a black woman who was a performer in France and she married a Frenchman and had six children, two boys and four girls. She was also talented. She was an entertainer and that is how she met my father. He was selling moonshine in the parking lot of the club she was performing in. My father had big ideas for his future. It did not include working for an honest day's pay. He wanted to be in charge of any criminal activity in the area. He was twenty-two and my mother was twenty. As time went on, they got married shortly after they met. They both wanted the same things and one thing was to make big money.

"'My father was a good card player and won a lot of money playing poker. In fact, that is how he got his first juke joint. He won it in a card game from one of the local businessmen. He called it the Pico's Junction. He turned it into a place where you could, drink, eat, smoke Cuban cigars, enjoy the company of fast women, and purchase whatever type of drugs your heart desired. That was Pico Junction and that was my parents.

"'At some point, they became the major players in the drug culture of New Orleans. With law enforcement on their payroll, they became the go-to people. My mother was a very pretty, talented lady. She always carried herself like a lady. But she was vicious on the inside. She was far more dangerous than my father. There is no way of determining how many people she killed or had killed but no one crossed her. She did not believe in second chances.

"'My father followed her lead and was a willing partner in all her decisions. He killed his share of violators. My mother did not get pregnant with me until later in life. I was delivered by Cesarean Section and the doctor told her she needed to have an operation in order to stop the bleeding. Because of the operation, she would not be able to have any more children. That is when she allowed my father to start seeing and visiting the fast women of the club.

"'My next confession is about me. I have decided to change my ways and become a different person. How I will accomplish this, I do not know at this point. But it will happen. Eva has a law enforcement background and I am asking her not to report what I am about to say to the law. I will spend the rest of my life helping others and want a second chance,' said Zola.

"'We agree,' said Eva and Nick.

"'When I was nineteen, I killed a cop who was trying to rape me and my parents sent me out of town and I landed in Harrisonville, N.C. That is where I met Nick and Nate. My accountant who stole my life's saving was murdered on my orders. I have sold all kinds of drugs, was a madam in my own house of prostitution, and a few other things like gaming and loan sharking in my own private bank. In order to survive with all my baggage, I started drinking very heavily. I did not do drugs but it was not easy with my guilt about Janet, my baby, dying in the fire that was my fault. I abused my body by getting pregnant every year only to lose the baby at the end of nine months. Some of these babies did not belong to Nate but he never knew. Please do not tell him. I have been to hell and know I need to find a way to get to heaven one day.

"'This is my confession. I will be leaving shortly to go stay with my great aunt who is my grandmother's sister. She is seventy-six years old but in good health. She will help me sort things out and help me find myself. She is a devoted Christian woman. She lives in Lynnville, Alabama, and is waiting for my arrival. She told me to leave the kids with their father because he needed to learn how to be a real man.

"'Please give Nate this note and maybe someday our paths will meet again under better circumstances. I wish you two the very best for your upcoming marriage. Take a look at the criminal history of this family and raise your future children to lead and live a Christian life. I've got to go but my children will always be in my heart and mind,' said Zola.

"As Nate read the note, tears ran down his eyes. The tears fell on the note and faded out some of Zola's words but they were now etched in his mind forever.

"Nate wanted Nick to know what was in the note. 'Dear love, I have let you down many times throughout the years. It is time that I leave and allow you and the children to live a life that is without a lost soul like me. Hopefully, I will be able to find myself and become a better person. Please do not attempt to look for me. I need to be able to rest my corrupt soul and reclaim my life. I have given it to the devil. I will always love you and the kids. I have to leave in order to save us all and with love in my heart, Zola,' said Nate.

"Nate slowly tore up the note, turned, and walked out of the house. It appeared he was in a daze. Nick caught up with him. 'Nick, how did all this happen to me and my family?' asked Nate.

'Well, Nate, do not blame yourself. It all started long before we were born. Criminal activity started with our grandparents or maybe great-grandparent. We were introduced to it at an early age, but at some point, we made our own decisions as to what we wanted,' said Nick.

"'I am leaving, Nick. Years ago when the babies were born, you and Eva became the godparents. At that time, we asked the two of you to take care of our children if we're not able. Well, I am leaving and giving them to you. I will sign a paper giving you custody of Toto and Lola. I am not worthy of raising children. I have a criminal mind. These children need someone they can depend on every day. I am going to get in my car and take off. Everything I have here, I want it put in trust for them. I will send you a P.O. Box address to mail the paper. Please do this for me. They deserve a chance in life. With me as their father, it might not happen,' said Nate.

"The next day, Nate gave both children a big hug and told them that their mother was gone away to get well. 'She will be back someday, but until then your Uncle Nick is going to take care of you because I have to leave. Today you do not understand but one day you will understand. Your mother and I love you today, tomorrow, and forever,' said Nate.

"Nick got up early the next morning to try to convince Nate not to go, but he was gone. The kids were now thirteen and Nick did not know that they were young criminals. This was the beginning of the third generation of criminals," said Lola.

"How did you feel without a mother or father?" asked Ted.

"It was a very low period in my brother's life and my life. Because of our parents' lack of supervision, we were raising ourselves. I recall when Toto was about three years old and our parents were having a party at our home and he got into my mother's jug of homemade cough syrup. I can't say for sure but I believe Toto was born an alcoholic. Even I love to drink. My mother loved wine and beer, and she must have been drinking when she was pregnant with us.

"That night, Toto had passed out. Mom came into the room to check on us. Toto was shooting a stream of pee straight up in the air. She took one look at him and knew what had happened. I had a few sips and was very dizzy but not out. Toto was out. I told her that we were coughing and needed the syrup. She was not happy. She did not know that Toto was stealing sips of her wine and beer whenever she left it unattended. Sometimes he would steal the drinks of their guests. Toto didn't care whose drink it was. He wanted it and he got it," said Lola.

"Drinking, to him, was like having a bottle of milk. Toto was very smart, good-looking, a great athlete, and tall for his age, with light brown skin and bedroom eyes. That was my brother and I love him. As he got older, he was very popular among his circle of friends. I remember, in fourth grade, seeing him on the playground selling cigarettes, which he stole from my father, to the older kids or anyone with money. He did not need money but it was the excitement of doing it that was pleasing to him. He smoked and drank and wanted company," said Lola.

"Toto loved sports and started playing little league, running track, basketball, and tennis. He was good at all of them. He was the only kid on any of these teams that was drunk the night before and was the most valuable player the next day," said Lola.

"Eva started planning her wedding and it was to take place in the fall of the next year. Meanwhile, I was having my problems. I saw what Toto was doing and decided to stay straight and not drink or smoke. I needed to watch out for Toto. Uncle Nick believed that we were good kids. After Eva and Uncle Nick got married, they purchased a big, nice home in New Orleans and we all moved from the boathouse to the new home. In the new home, we had our own living quarters. It consisted of two bedrooms, an activity room, two bathrooms, and a small kitchen.

"My uncle and Eva were very wealthy but worked every day to help others. My uncle had his own law firm for low-income residents and Eva was his office manager. Sometimes they would represent important people. They worked for long hours during the week. Therefore, once again we were raising ourselves," said Lola.

"I took up music and dance in high school and excelled quickly with my talent. My great-grandmother, grandmother, and mother were entertainers and that is what I wanted. I was always the lead performer in all the musicals at school.

"Toto decided to stick with football, which he did not start playing until the coach discovered him during gym in his freshmen year of high school. Being a smart businessman, he knew he could find more clients on the football field than on the playground," said Lola.

"'Toto, your position is wide receiver. You are an athlete. You are quick, aggressive, smart with your moves, and can figure out how to catch the ball. There are other positions you could play but that is what I need this year,' said the coach.

"Toto thought to himself, 'In this position, I have to be sober but I can sell wine to the defense. They will be awesome. They will be feared. We will win the state championship for the next four years.'

"My uncle and Eva were at all our events and were very proud of us. We got good grades and were always on the honor roll. Something was happening to Toto that was uncontrollable. Even I was becoming different," said Lola.

"Our special section of the house was becoming very popular with the teenagers in town. At first, we would ask our uncle if we could have some friends over. This was the beginning of our decision to follow the family tradition of being professional criminals. We came up with reasons to have a party. Our uncle never said no. They loved us and we were nice kids. We had chores at home and were popular at school. Even the teachers liked us. We were model students," said Lola.

"With the parties, we needed booze. So my brother would find a bum and give him a few dollars with a list of alcohol to purchase. Toto and his friends would wait in parking lot at the local diner to make the exchange. I started wearing makeup and started keeping myself pretty. The guys loved me but I was not interested. I wanted to wait for the man of my dreams. But Toto was completely opposite. He would have sex with anyone. He would often state, 'I don't care if they are blind, crippled, or crazy. A woman is a woman.' And that is how he lived his life. On the edge of danger," said Lola.

"Toto decided to start inviting adults to our weekly parties. My uncle and Eva would also come to make sure there was enough food. I loved to play the piano and sing, and Toto was good at playing by ear, singing, and dancing. One of my parents' best friend, Spook Jackson, would often stop by and play his sax. The Blues was on every Saturday night.

"Eva wanted us to enjoy the house and moved our Saturday night parties into their main ballroom. This was the beginning of opening of a whole different can of worms," said Lola.

"Did your parents ever try to contact you or your brother?" asked Ted.

"They send birthday and Christmas cards with gifts," responded Lola.

"Having Saturday night parties turned into a regular thing and the neighborhood became standard guest. Spook Jackson and Slap the Hog, alone with Toto and I were the main entertainers. Spook played the sax and Slap the Hog played the piano. I danced and sang jazz songs. Toto did it all but he loved women and liquor.

"Consuming, buying, and selling liquor was Toto's main objective in high school. As a member of the team, he played wide receiver and understood that in order to be good in that position, he had to be sober. He also realized that the offensive and defensive line would be fearless with a little help from the bottle. Therefore, before each game, Toto would sell moonshine that he learned to make from people like Spook. Spook was his partner in name only. Spook was well aware of what Toto was capable of doing.

"Toto's liquor business got so big that he recruited me to work with him. Spook owned several acres of land and that is where Toto set up his stills. The moonshine sales had a special target market. This market was mainly of teenagers and college students.

"The football team's coach knew what Toto was doing but turned his head as long as the Silver Nights were undefeated. The defense was so good that their opponents looked defeated as they entered the football field. The team practiced hard and played the game even harder. During half-time, the coach and the offensive and defensive linesmen would take a shot of corn liquor. When they entered the field, the score would be so lop-sided in their favor that they would just go through the motions.

Toto's young years were where he learned to be a professional criminal. Professional because he was smart and understood how to work with people, compassionate, and could figure out how to solve issues and come up with great solutions. His first real test was on the football field. A team from up North wanted to play the Silver Nights because of their reputation. This northern team also had a reputation. They had been undefeated for two seasons and had become nationally known. The news stations had featured them several times on T.V. When asked how they became so good, the coach would reply, 'Hard work with reliable dedicated players,'" said Lola.

"Toto said to the coach, 'I want this team to feel welcomed. I would like to have an early afternoon party for them. The menu will be Bar-B-Q ribs and chicken, corn on the cob, potato salad, greens, and baked beans. I will serve punch, soda, and water with homemade peach cobbler. This way, we can get to know this fearless team before we play with them.'

"'Good,' said the coach, 'but no funny stuff in the punch.'

"Without responding, Toto just smiled.

"My uncle and aunt were so happy that they were reaching out to this team of minority players. They felt good about how we were being raised.

"This northern team was made up of a bunch of city slickers. They were just a few steps away from being criminals. Toto had done his research on this team and the coach. He discovered that they came from a part of the city that was infested with gangs. Many of them were former gang members. These kids were ordered by the courts to join a sport or activity in their school while on probation or go into a detention facility. Knowing this information, Toto decided to put his best moonshine in a special punch bowl. The team captain was told about the special bowl and the word spread among his team like a wildfire. It did not matter if the Silver Nights drank this punch because it was like lemonade to them. If they came out to play sober, they would lose all their games. Drunk was the only way they played," said Lola.

"The teams ate and drank everything. Nothing was left. Everyone had a good time. When the sun was going down, everyone was invited into the ballroom to finish off the party. Toto got on the piano and started playing and I sang the best R&B songs that were popular at that time. The party was on and so was the game.

"Toto said to me, 'May they eat, drink, and be happy because tomorrow they will be losers!'

"Sure enough, they were losers. Not just losers but shut out. Score was 21 to 0. What an embarrassment! I felt bad for this team and now the Silver Nights were featured on the evening news for shutting this northern team down. That is how Toto plays the criminal game. Study your enemy and then design a winning game plan.

"Toto lay in bed that evening with a big smile on his face. He knew he had out-slicked the city slickers. 'I am the greatest,' Toto shouted over and over again. 'Tomorrow will bring new opportunities and challenges and I am ready for them all!' said Toto, speaking out loud.

"On Monday morning, I was sick and my aunt suggested that I stay home from school. God must have been on Toto's side because the school called the house and I answered the phone," said Lola.

"'Mrs. Harrison, this is the school nurse; Toto has a small bottle of something that smells like it has liquor in it. He said it is your homemade version of cough syrup. He was caught with it in his history class. If that is true, he needs to give me a note telling me how often and how much to give him during the day,' said the nurse.

"Yes, everything he told you was right. I gave him my homemade cough syrup because he did not want to miss school. He has had perfect attendance every year since kindergarten and did not want to mess up his record," said Lola.

"We were doing great and our liquor sales were growing and getting larger. In fact, a few friends of Toto were hired to help with the making of moonshine. After football season was over, Toto and I had to find other places to sell our liquor. It did not take long. We started attending the Friday night dances at our school and other nearby high schools. We doubled our supply and would sell out before the dance was over.

"Toto was tested once again. He was still a freshman but a wise one. At one of the dances at our school, Maria, who was very popular with Toto and some of the other guys, loved to dance. She was just the right partner for Toto. He was not just a lover but a dancer too. At this dance, he offered Maria some moonshine and she gladly accepted. She was a good-looking girl but no one but her cousin knew she was epileptic. She drank the liquor straight down and within seconds, she started having a seizure. She was yelling, 'Demo, Demo!'" said Lola.

"'I am Demo. I am Demo!' yelled Toto.

"Everyone was scared. Toto got a cold glass of water and threw in Maria's face. She stopped shaking and all her seizure activity stopped. After that, Toto was known as Demo. The word traveled quickly and that was his new nickname. Demo was a better name than Toto," said Lola.

"After what happened to Maria, Demo focused his sales at schools and on Saturday nights in the ballroom. Summer had arrived and Demo and I were honor roll students entering into the tenth grade. That summer was unbelievable. Every day was full of excitement. Ladies of all ages loved Demo and men of all ages loved me. Demo engaged in liquor and women but I just loved to look good and be nice but no sex.

"My uncle and aunt felt that something was going on but could not put their fingers on it. Every good thing has to come to an end at some point. The end was near when the cleaning lady, who was a wino, approached Demo for sex. She was about sixty years old but thought she was still a looker. Two years ago, she was hit by a car on the major highway in town and my uncle handled her case. She was drunk when she got hit while crossing the street. She did not get much money. In the accident, she lost her leg. Her name was Maggie.

"My uncle felt sorry for her and invited her to live with them and become the head housekeeper. She not only was the head housekeeper but the head of the house drunks. Demo thought it would be cool to have sex with a one-legged woman," said Lola.

"Maggie knew no one was home and would not take 'no' for an answer. It did not take much for Demo to comply. As they were going at it and unaware that my uncle and aunt had come home and were looking for Demo, after calling and looking, they decided to check into Maggie's quarters. As they entered her living room, there were Demo and Maggie rolling all over the floor.

"My aunt screamed and fainted. It was a sight to see. Maggie was asked to leave and Demo was under house arrest. This did not stop Demo. His summer was just beginning," said Lola.

"'Lola, we will be sixteen in a few weeks and will be able to get our driver's license. Hopefully Uncle Nick will buy us a car,' said Demo.

"'If you watch yourself and keep a low profile, maybe he will. Because of our criminal genes, he wants to make sure we live an honest life. Sorry Uncle, it is too late. We are criminals and loving it,' I responded.

"My uncle gave us driving lessons because he felt that everyone should know how to drive even if they did not have anything to drive. We needed their license in case of an emergency," said Lola.

"One hot summer's early evening, some of our buddies wanted to go roller-skating but no one had any transportation. My uncle and aunt were out of town and were scheduled to return in the morning," said Lola.

"'I know, I will use my uncle's Mercedes and he will never know it. We need some liquor to take with us. I will ask Maggie to go get us some booze from Blank's liquor store. I will have to buy her a pint of wine. She is an old fool but a good fuck,' said Demo.

"Nick and Eva were beginning to realize what they were raising and decided to get some professional help. They had planned to take us to a child therapist on Monday morning when they returned home," said Lola.

"We had a good time at the skating rink. We sat in the car after skating and drank our liquor. Demo was in no shape to drive, so Ken, the driver, offered to drive. He was drunker than Demo, so I was the driver. I was also drunk.

"We were almost home when I passed out. The car ran up on our neighbor's lawn and landed in her living room. No one was hurt but we were all passed out. The local newspaper came and took pictures. This town had never had anyone's car end up in someone's living room. The headlines read, *Teenagers, drunk and all underage landed in neighbor's living room after a night of drinking*," said Lola.

"The cops took us to the hospital to check us out. It was hard to tell who was driving because no one was behind the wheel. The police asked but we could not remember. I was so scared that my pants were soaking wet. Demo was cool. He had a story; he told the truth.

"His truth was that we all stole the car. That was his truth; he stole the car and dragged us along. My uncle was very upset and the first thing on Monday morning was that we were sitting in the therapist's office," said Lola.

"The therapist was given a complete history of the Harrison family and after talking to us alone, without my uncle, she said, 'I will see all of you in four weeks and I will have a report which will outline the problems and a plan to rehabilitate these two teenagers. During summer vacation, they should be in a summer camp, one that builds values such as learning to improve on a sport or learning a sport or learning a foreign language.'

'That night, my uncle wrote out a contract that he read to us and required us to sign. He did not know that Demo and I were alcoholics. He soon found out the hard way," said Lola.

"'This is your contract.

I will keep my room clean.

I will do my own laundry.

I will help with the yard work.

I will attend a summer camp.

I will give up all access to any money or allowances.

I will not have any company or Saturday night parties.

Lola Harris _____

Demo Harris _____

Date: _____ "

said Uncle Nick.

"Just to be on the safe side, my uncle removed all liquor so that we did not have our Saturday night parties for the neighborhood. Money was never an issue but this caused a serious problem for us. We were alcoholics and loved to smoke cigarettes, and without any money we were doomed," said Lola.

"Demo got in touch with Spook Jackson and asked him to start up the stills.

"'I have a few bucks saved for hard times and this is the time to reinvest. We need to start right away. Lola and I will be at a summer camp during the day, but in the evening we will be able to help. I will work on developing clients at the camp.

Most of the campers are from our high school and they will be ready for some refreshments,' said Demo.

"This was a camp for teenagers who were interested in learning a foreign language. We enrolled in two classes, Spanish and French. Demo figured we would be exposed to more kids who would become clients," said Lola.

"Yes, he was right. Demo was a born salesman along with his other gifts. Not only was he selling to the campers but he was also selling to selected staff. He knew who to sell to. He was back in business and I loved it.

"Our criminal empire started at camp. Johnny, the camp nerd, bumped into Demo. 'Oh excuse me, you are Demo Harrison. I have seen you at school. You are a cool guy. I have watched you operate. I run a small operation at school but nothing like yours. I deal with black market cigarettes and Cuban cigars. To get to the point, I can be a big asset to you in helping you grow your business into a larger business. You have the looks and the business brains in order for us to move forward. I am not scared of no one or nothing.'

"My uncle in New Orleans has many connections; even law enforcement is on his payroll. He is a leftover from the last big mobster boss who was killed years ago and his wife committed suicide in order to keep from going to jail, and maybe for life. 'If we join forces, I will take care of any rough stuff. That was my uncle's job before he became the boss. How about it? Do we have a deal?' asked Johnny.

"'Well, just a few questions, did this old boss have a daughter? If so, what was her name?' responded Demo.

"'Yes, I believe her name was Zola or something like that,' said Johnny.

"'That's interesting. Okay, we have a deal. After camp, let's get together at my house. My uncle will love you because you look honest and have the looks of a good citizen,' said Demo.

"'That's what makes me good at what I do. My looks are an asset and do not give me away,' said Johnny.

"That evening, Johnny came to dinner and my uncle and aunt just loved him. All three of us were 'A' students. We were all the bright lights of the school. Success was our final destination in life. Little did they know that being a great criminal was our final destination," said Lola.

"Lola, you do remember that I am not the lead lawyer on your case, only the assistant. Based on what you have told me, this case is more than about you. It is about a long line of criminals from way back. Your case is going to solve many unsolved cases. The FBI will have to come in at some point. We will ask for total immunity for you and any family members that are still alive. How does that sound?" asked Ted.

"That sounds good, but with what I have told you so far, how are my chances of getting off?" asked Lola.

"If what you told me holds up, this is a slam dunk. The court will not know what hit them," responded Ted.

"Okay, let's get back because the good stuff is about to start," said Lola.

Ted looked at Lola and realized she was the woman of his dreams if he could get her off and she became an honest lady. 'I believe after this was over, she would be a new person,' Ted thought to himself.

"Ted, there is a lot more. Demo and I developed our own network of criminal activity. It did not take long. By the time we were entering college, we had a team assembled that were experts in their special chosen careers. Johnny handled all the merchandize deliveries. Henry was the bookkeeper and accountant. Leroy was the enforcer. Spook was in charge of growing the corn on his twenty-five-acre farm that was used in the making of the corn liquor. Stump was responsible for distributions and management of his clients. Demo and I overlooked the total operation, made adjustments as needed, and kept the law off our backs. All decisions were made by Demo and me. We were the owners and they were the staff. Demo made it quite clear that we were the bosses.

"With Johnny as part of our operation, we were able to add the black market cigarettes. My uncle and aunt started to be concerned about us. All summer during camp, we were selling to the campers and many of the young adults who were college students. Henry was a freshman college student who was a camp counselor. He spoke several languages and was here from France on a student visa. He needed money for college and his off-campus apartment. He was perfect for the organization. Instead of an apartment, we rented him a large, older home consisting of five acres and a basement. This became our headquarters.

"Leroy was the leader of one of the biggest gangs in town. He was excellent in his role because he was good at ruffling people up. Moreover, he also had his own group. This was the management team for our organization. All we needed was a name, the Redds after my grandfather who would have been proud of us," said Lola.

"How did Demo and you know how to put together a criminal organization of this magnitude? You were just kids, high school kids," said Ted.

"We had help," responded Lola.

"When my uncle took custody of us, we moved off his boathouse and into a big home. One day, my brother and I were playing in the basement and ran across some boxes that were labeled: Redd and Nina Harrison, Candee and Buddy, and

Frank. We recognized our grandparents' names but the other names did not mean much. As we opened all the boxes, it was like reliving history. These boxes told the whole story. My grandfather was the narrator. His words were just popping off the pages.

"Someone had put them in order as much as possible by dates beginning in the early 1900s. It was my uncle because he was the lawyer in the family. These boxes had tape recording, journals, diaries, deeds, pictures, and basic notebooks. Their accountant had made an organizational chart listing everyone's title. His ledger included things like how much money was being collected daily, weekly, monthly, and yearly. The records were excellent.

"The pictures were labeled with names, places, and dates. We figured that my grandmother was the picture lady. There was also another set of boxes labeled: Zola's family, FBI. We decided not to open it, but we needed to know both sides of the family. We were only about twelve at the time but were very aggressive and smart. On every Saturday and Sunday afternoon, we would go to the basement to play. We even had our games set up like we were playing but we were reading every scrap of paper and we also listened to the tapes that were made by the state attorney general's office about our grandparents and their associates.

"That is when Demo and I decided that it would be more exciting to be criminals than to work in an office from nine to five," said Lola

"Everything we needed to know was in those boxes. It was a road map of how to become a criminal and be good at it. They were good. But at the end, they died. Well, no one will live forever. Maybe we should all just do what makes us happy. For Demo and me, criminal life is our only life. It makes us happy. Both parents skipped out on us and my wonderful uncle was left to raise us two criminals," said Lola.

"Have you ever thought about your future of being an honest person or what else you could do to make your life complete and happy?" asked Ted.

"Reading my grandmother's diary, it was obvious that she was truly in love with my grandfather from the first time they met. She wanted to have a family so badly that she disregarded the doctor's advice, which was to not get pregnant. Her health was bad, and with her diabetes, it could be fatal. As you know it was. I would like to be in love like that and have a large family. I would like to give something to the community. In college, I majored in science with most of my courses in chemistry. I would like to go back to school and get a PhD in chemistry and open my laboratory someday. At twenty-four, I am still young enough to start over," said Lola.

"When we get you off from all of these charges, maybe you will have a shot at all your dreams. When did your uncle and aunt finally discover your criminal activities?" asked Ted.

"The summer of us going into our senior year in high school is when it finally hit them in the face. They first discovered that Demo was a juvenile alcoholic. Demo never drank during the week, but on Friday evening, he was ready for action. He would mix moonshine with coke, walking around all night with a glass of coke in his hand. This continued all weekend. Our grades were outstanding in school, which threw them off. Demo had many years of drinking and he was able to drink without getting drunk," said Lola.

"One Saturday night, Demo and his buddies from the neighborhood went roller-staking in a town about ten miles away. By this time, my uncle had purchased a car for both of us. They were used cars but nice. I had a black Chevy Impala and Demo's car was a red Ford Crown Victoria convertible. The guys in the town, where the skating rink was located, had sent word to Demo and his friends that they were not welcomed in their town and talking to their girls. Demo believed he was invincible and no one could hurt him or do harm. He had his organization behind him. After skating was over, they had a dance and that is when Demo got a wake-up call.

"Demo was a tall, good-looking black guy. He was a great dancer and he had his booze with him in his coke bottle. His buddies also had booze in a bottle. As the music got good and Demo started showing off this dancing abilities, the girls were lining up and would not dance with no one but Demo. It was Demo's show, just like old times with his mother," said Lola.

"The guys from the town started gathering in small groups and were eyeing down the outsiders. One of the leaders came up to Demo and said, 'You should clear out now while you can go home with both of your eyes.'

"His buddies were not fighters; they wanted to be players. Many of them had never been in a fight. They were Demo's social friends and best customers. All during the dance, Demo and his friends were the only ones the girls would dance with. If they could not get Demo, they would take one of his friends. After the dance was over and Demo and his buddies were leaving with a few girls, the action started. Demo was in the backseat with his girl and his three buddies were standing outside the car. A local gang with tire irons and baseball bats charged at them. Without much notice, the buddies were on the ground.

"The gang was kicking them and yelling, 'Go back to Squaresville, you fucking hicks! Leave our girls alone. If you come back, we'll kill you.'

"They pulled Demo out the car and beat up on him. Next, they smashed up the car. Even the roof was almost missing. The only thing that saved them that night from more torture was that one of the workers at the skating rink called the police. The police took all of them to the hospital. My uncle was called," said Lola.

"'Mr. Harrison, this is the Laurence Police Department. We have your nephew here at the police station along with his three friends. They were in a fight with a local gang. They were beaten up very badly but they will survive. We took them to the hospital and got them medical attention. They have many cuts that required stitches. They were intoxicated and had liquor on them. They need an adult to pick them up or they will have to go to jail. Your nephew's car was totaled,' said the officer.

"My uncle called the other boys' parents and had them to pick up their kids. My uncle was totally shocked; he did not know what to do. He knew, after Demo had stolen his car and wrecked it several years ago, that Demo had some problems but without any other situation over the years, he believed that going to camp that summer cured him," said Lola.

"Demo looked awful; he had cuts all over his forehead, broken jaw, and bruised ribs. Both of his eyes were shut tight. I almost did not recognize my brother. The car was totaled. It was a pile of junk," said Lola.

"The next day, my uncle and aunt sat both of us down. 'Please tell us what is going on. We love you now and forever. We are family and want to help,' said Uncle Nick.

"Demo and I had already decided to tell the truth, with a few things left out," said Lola.

"'We are both alcoholics. If I had been sober and just went to skate and dance, none of this would have happened. Trust me; this will not happen ever again. We want to go to AA for juvenile alcoholics. After last night, I escaped death and don't want to go down that path again. We have been alcoholics for many years. It all started with our parents and the fact that liquor was always around. When we had a cold, Mom would give us her homemade cough syrup. It was made out of corn liquor. We learned to love it and would steal it whenever we could. They never caught on to us,' said Demo.

"'Okay, that's the plan. When you recover from last night, you two will start your program. I will set it up for you two,' responded Uncle Nick.

"While Demo was recovering from his night of awareness, I took over the organization. I had a different way of operating. Leroy came to me and wanted to sell drugs in our market. In my grandfather's papers, it was clear that drugs were prohibited. He believed that they harmed kids, families, and destroyed lives. Demo and I believed the same. I told Leroy that would be his decision and his business because I did not want anything to do with drugs. He started selling the next day," said Lola.

"In my grandparents' papers, they had spoken about the different services they offered clients. The gambling and Gentlemen's Basement were very appealing to me. Many college students needed money for college and this would be a good way to earn it. Many of them were giving it away for free, so now it was time to make it pay off.

"I decided to call it Zola's Room. There was an outstanding description of the Gentlemen's Basement. Therefore I coped with Zola's Room after the Gentlemen's Basement. The rental house basement was just right for it. I turned the dining room and living room into poker rooms. Poker is very popular on college campuses. I believe where there is a need or want, someone will eventually fill that need. I was the right person," said Lola.

"It took Demo all summer to recover from his injuries. He would ask me how things were going and I would respond, 'Just great.' I wanted to surprise him. Money was never our motivation. We had money. It was power, influence, control, and to grow up and be just like our grandparents. That is what it did for us. The other members of our organization, they needed the money. We never allowed them to know that we were wealthy. Demo and I believed that if they knew, they might resent us," said Lola.

"Demo recovered just in time to go back to school, for it was our senior year and we wanted to graduate in a dead heat for number-one in our class. Demo was the class president for all four years and I was the vice president for all four years. He was perfect for that job. He was truly a leader. He could have been a leader in any occupation," said Lola.

"Demo was back to playing football. He was a wide receiver. He never drank while playing, for he wanted to be the best with a great offensive line to work with him. The team was undefeated for three years. The moonshine he sold the defense made them play like animals. In fact, their nickname was 'The Animals.'

"Just before school started, Demo dropped by the house which was now called Off Campus. Demo's eyes opened wide as he entered the house. He yelled, "This is wonderful! What a place! Students can come here to relax and have fun without fear of getting locked up. Great name, Off Campus,' said Demo.

"I'm glad you like it," responded Lola.

"Did Demo and you stay out of trouble with the law during your senior year?" asked Ted.

"As long as we were going to our AA meeting, we were somewhat okay. I could see some changes in Demo, but I was not able figure it out. He would always speak at AA and tell it all. He had found another place to take over," said Lola.

"'My name is Kevin Harrison but my friends call me Demo.' Demo sounded better than Kevin. It was more fitting for a teenage alcoholic. I have been an alcoholic before I was potty-trained. It started with my mother giving me her homemade cough syrup. I enjoyed faking a cough so that I could get the cough syrup which was made with moonshine. After that, I would just help myself to it when my parents were not around. Later, it got so controlling that I took it to school and drank it in the bathroom during the changing of the classes.

"'I got caught just once at school. But that did not stop me. Later, I stole my wonderful uncle's car and destroyed it by running into a house and landing in the front living room. I was drunk. I was a drunk. I believe God was on my side, for I should have been dead with all that alcohol in my system in all those young years. Maybe God is saving me for something bigger. Who knows? I am still alive and well. Let's end my talk with Amazing Grace,' said Demo.

"I said to Demo, 'Are you a fake, faking this entire AA stuff or are you playing it straight?'

"'I am not sure. The words just come out of my mouth,' said Demo.

"It was at that moment that I knew Demo would not be a criminal all his life. This was just getting ready for something bigger. What, when, where, and how he would change might be revealed someday," said Lola.

"The football team went undefeated in our senior year and most of the team members were seniors. The coach knew that a team like this only comes along once in a lifetime and the

Demos of the world were rare. The state championship was on the radio. My Uncle Nick invited the neighbors over on a first-come basis to listen to the game in the ballroom while we went to the game.

The Silver Nights won by three points. 17 to 14, a field goal was kicked with ten seconds left on the clock. Demo had delivered two touchdowns and a field goal by his buddy in crime, the kicker," said Lola.

"Did you two stop drinking and get ready for college?" asked Ted.

"We slowed down a little but we were still drunks. As I look back, I believe it might have been because we missed our parents. The organization was going good and I decided to start giving out my own student loans. I remember reading in my grandparents' papers that they had a bank. This bank's function was to loan money at high interest rates. Our student clients did not qualify for traditional bank loans and most of them just wanted some extra pocket change.

"Henry, the bookkeeper, was to run the bank. He would receive sixty percent of all interest collected. Henry was good at his job and decided to major in accounting. He was getting plenty of experience from the Redds," said Lola.

"Did your parents come to your high school graduation?" asked Ted.

"No," said Lola.

"That's it? Just no?" responded Ted.

"Let's move on," said Lola.

"Demo and I were named co-valedictorians of the graduating class. After the ceremony, we went to several parties. Everyone wanted us at their party, even their parents. We were wasted. I was driving my black Chevy Impala and Demo said, 'Let's rob Tony's Liquor Store.'

"Everyone agreed and that is what we did. We took a hammer and knocked out the front window display and took all the display liquor and then stepped inside and stole all the best stuff. Off we went to our headquarters. Before we got to a half block down the road, Officer Jones put on his siren and pulled us over. He pulled up and Demo put a bottle of Clevis Regal out and offered Officer Jones a drink," said Lola.

"'Get out of the car and all of you get into my car,' ordered Officer Jones.

"It was late, about 2:00 a.m. My uncle knew we would be home late because of all the parties. He did throw the book at us before we went out partying," said Lola.

"'No drinking or smoking dope. If you get into trouble and get picked by the cops, don't call me. We are done with that nonsense. We managed to get the two of you through school alive and now you need to act like adults. Remember, don't call me,' said Nick.

"I told Officer Jones not to call my uncle but he did anyway," said Lola.

"'This is Officer Jones. I just picked up a bunch of drunken kids and two of them belong to you. They robbed Tony's Liquor Story. Do you want to come and get yours? They are not eighteen years old yet,' said the officer.

"'You got them. You keep them. I will see you in the morning,' responded Nick.

"Spending a night in jail with a bunch of drunken kids and bums was awful. It was smelly and wet. This should have been a wakeup call for me but it wasn't," said Lola.

"As my Uncle Nick walked into the police station and was escorted to the holding cell where all of us were, it was obvious that he had a disgusting look on his face.

"'I have been there for the two of you all your life. I was in the hospital when you were born. I have loved you before your mother gave birth to both of you. I do not understand why you two are the way you are. It must be in the genes.

"'It could be a family curse. Only God knows. I still love you and will fight for your life, for you to live it as honest, productive citizens of this great country,' said Nick.

"Demo and I looked at each other in shame but I could see that Demo was truly upset with himself. I just did not understand how upset he was with his life," said Lola.

"'Lola, I am going back to AA, and this time I plan to live up to my commitment to stay sober. I feel good when I am sober. I cannot blame my alcohol condition on anyone but myself. It might have started with Mom but it has to end with me. From this day on, I want to be called by my birth name Kevin. Kevin sounds like a name for a nice young man who wants something in life,' said Demo.

"Like my parents, I liked the power and the ability to control others. It was totally a gene thing. That summer was the beginning of a new life for me. Kevin was still my partner but in name only. I was always out and he stuck around the house, working in the garden and helping anywhere there was a need.

"My focus was mainly on the business and getting organized the way I had dreamed. I was proud of being a young entrepreneur. Kevin was at the point where he wanted to stay away from any place that involved alcohol. I had also stopped drinking but still loved the business.

"I added a few improvements. We now had a menu that included chicken wings, hot dogs, chilly, chips, non-alcoholic drinks, and moonshine. I hired a few waitresses who wore uniforms that looked like swimsuits. They included a cook, a bouncer,

a bartender, a girl to run the Gentlemen's Basement, and poker dealers who worked Friday evenings until 3:00 a.m., Saturdays from 6:00 p.m. to 3:00 a.m., and Sundays 3:00 p.m. until 11:00 p.m. We were closed from Monday to Thursday. I wanted the students to study on those days and go to classes.

"That summer business got so busy that we had to issue membership cards. The cards cost $5.00. It was good until we finished college. I also had a couple of parking lot attendants. The cars were directed into the woods. I now employed about twenty young people," said Lola.

"Things were going great until I caught Leroy selling dope in the parking lot of the club.

"'Leroy, you agreed not to sell here at the club. This is my business. That dope is your business. Sell it on the streets or anywhere but not here!' I yelled.

"Leroy took one look at me and said, 'I will sell at any fucking place I want to sell, madam.'

"I had my bouncer with me and he had a gun. 'Look here, dirtbag. You heard Lola. Stop selling and leave and do not return,' said my bouncer.

"'Our business relationship is over. Don't come around anymore,' I said.

"It was a few days before we started college. My uncle and aunt wanted to take Kevin and me out for dinner to celebrate our departure for college. My uncle was very proud of us because Kevin was in AA and I did not appear to be getting into any trouble all summer. My uncle thought that both of us had been reborn and were now honest adults," said Lola.

"'I have something to tell you, Lola. I want you to understand that I love you but I will be going to a different college. This way, we will learn to be independent. I have been accepted into UCLA and will be leaving tomorrow. I need my space. I need to find out if I have what it takes to be my own person. I hope you understand,' said Kevin.

"It was hard at first not having Kevin around but after a few weeks at the local university, I was back to my old self. That is, studying and managing the Off Campus Club.

"I decided to major in business because it would fit right in with my club. In school, I met Ricky and we started hanging out together. He was also a business major. At first, I did not want to let him know that I was the owner of Off Campus Club because I felt it would ruin our relationship. Ricky already knew, for he was a steady customer of Kevin in high school, even though he went to a different school. Ricky said he never met my brother but would buy his moonshine, cigarettes, and dope from Leroy," said Lola.

"Ricky was very handsome and fun to be around. We were spending a great deal of time together. Therefore, I decided to move out of my uncle's home and move into the club. My uncle did not know this rented house was a college nightclub. My uncle and aunt were busy traveling and enjoying themselves now that we were grown. They believed it was their time," said Lola.

"I did not see or hear from Kevin until Thanksgiving. He told the family he needed time to develop a new life. My uncle invited many family members, mostly on my grandmother's side. As I told you before, my great-grandmother was black and, while performing in France, fell in love with a Frenchman and married him.

"The ballroom was full and my cousins were happy to be invited for dinner. We have never tried to keep it a secret that our family was of mixed heritage. Most people in the area knew it. It was never an issue with my uncle and aunt or our friends or in their professional life.

"Ricky entered the ballroom with me and it was decorated beyond belief. A perfect Christmas tree, red and white poinsettias inside and out, and all five tables set like something from better homes and gardens. Ricky was totally impressed. As he looked around, he noticed that the blacks outnumbered the white guests. At that point, he did not say anything. Kevin had not arrived yet. As we were escorted to our table, I could see from the look on his face that something was wrong. But I could not figure it out. Our family had many black and white friends. The color of their skin was not important; it was what was in their heart," said Lola.

"At our table was my uncle and aunt, Mr. Stevenson and his girlfriend, Uncle Nick's first cousin and her husband, and Ricky and me, and a seat reserved for Kevin. Kevin was coming in from California and was expected to be a little late. When Kevin walked into the ballroom, everyone stood up and clapped. He was still very handsome. His skin was a little tan from the California sun. He was slim, tall, and had a great smile. I grabbed him and took him to our table," said Lola.

"Ricky, this is my twin brother, Kevin," I said with a big, proud smile on my face.

"Ricky stood up and said, 'This is a black family and all these black people are your relatives. I have been dating a black girl. I will be a laughing stock among all my friends.'

"He left and just walked out of my life that day and even transferred to another university outstate the next semester. I never saw or heard from him again," said Lola.

"With or without Ricky, we had a great dinner and evening. After dinner, Kevin got on the baby grand piano and sang and played some popular songs. Many of the cousins were very talented and wanted to play their instruments or sing or dance. My aunt decided that we would have talent night. She made up a list of the guests that wanted to perform and she introduced them. There were solos, family groups, musicians, and dancers. It was a lot of fun.

"Even though most of guests were drinking wine or beer, Kevin only had ice tea. I followed his lead and drank ice tea all night," said Lola.

"What a Thanksgiving! How did you feel about Ricky after he exposed his racism?" asked Ted.

"I was very hurt. He was my very first boyfriend. I had dreamed it would be like my grandmother and grandfather, the way they felt the first time they set eyes on each other," said Lola.

"Kevin was going to leave on Sunday night to go back to school. Therefore, my uncle wanted to have a private talk with the two of us. Kevin and I did not know what the talk was going to be about, but we knew it would be serious," said Lola.

"'Your grandparents were loving people who believed in taking care of their children and families. Before you were born, they set up a trust fund for their grandchildren. It was to be divided equally among all the grandchildren and dispersed at age twenty-two. Eva and I have not been blessed with any children and you two are the only grandchildren from Redd and Nina. When you graduate from college, an account will set up in each of your names. It is a large sum. Please use it wisely and for a good cause," said Nick.

"With Ricky gone from my life, I was depressed for about a week, until I met up with my older cousin Belle who was about sixty-five. 'Let's go to lunch and catch up on old times,' I said.

"'Without Ricky, I feel lost. I just want to turn over and die,' I told my cousin.

"'Girl, you better straighten up and fly straight. That situation is a dead cat on a line. If my grandmother was alive, she would say, 'Let the hair go with the hide. You can't put your life in the hands of a man. You need to put your hands in the hands of the man who parted the sea. He will take care of you. Come to church on Sunday and let Him help,' said my Cousin Belle.

"As I lay in bed, I remembered my parents and how in love they were in the early years. What happened to them that made them two lost souls? Maybe if God had been invited into their lives, things would have turned out very differently. I hope wherever they are, they are happy and healthy. May God bless them and keep them safe until they return to us! This was my prayer that night," said Lola.

"My cousin was right. I needed to stop feeling depressed and get back into the swing of things again. I decided not to fall in love with anyone unless I interviewed them first. I would tell them that I was black. If they got through that comment, then we could go on with getting more involved.

"Back in school, I got deeply involved with the schoolwork and the Off Campus Café. I decided it needed a new look and a new owner. I was then twenty-one, and next year my trust fund was to come. I decided to buy the Café house. It looked rundown on the outside but was nice on the inside. I had done a lot of work that the owner did not know about. The owner lived out of state and never bothered to check on his investment. I never asked him to fix anything. My offer was to buy the house as it was. I had money saved from all the years from being in business. I put the money in a hidden safe in a false wall in my bedroom. Kevin had given me his share before he went off to college.

"For a few weeks, I sat down and jotted down some ideas. I wanted to expand and included more services. The bank was my little pet project. I made a contract for my clients. If they fell behind in their loan payments and were unable to catch up, they would have to work it off at the Off Campus Café until the debt was paid. If they did not pay or work off the debt, my debt collector would visit the client. I used an old friend of my grandparents' name, Bruce from New Orleans, who was good at scaring and collecting. Bruce was expensive and wanted to be paid monthly even if he did not have to collect. Bruce had his own organization. I informed Bruce that I could not have students borrowing from the bank and not planning on paying the bank back. He had my approval to do whatever it took to get justice but not to kill anyone or mane them for life. He agreed," said Lola.

"I purchased the house and my uncle and aunt were very proud of me. I told them that I was starting an Off Campus Café for college students and needed trust fund monies to make the necessary improvements. I said to them that I would be acquiring all the necessary license and permits in order to operate a restaurant, a dance hall, and over twenty-one bars that served beer and wine only. I got the permits for the improvements and necessary license for the restaurant and dance hall. I had no plans on giving up the Gentlemen's Basement, gambling, the bank, or serving moonshine. It was too profitable.

"My improvements included an addition to the building which would be my living space, new siding, a swimming pool with cabanas, and a complete renovation of the gambling room, restaurant, kitchen, dance hall, and Gentlemen's Basement," said Lola.

"My uncle loaned me the money until my trust fund kicked in. Everything was going great. The students were having fun and it was the place to go to on the weekends. I graduated from college as a business major and Kevin graduated too. My graduation was first, so my uncle and aunt came to my graduation. We flew out to UCLA for Kevin's graduation. He was the valedictorian of his class with a major in theology. It was announced that Kevin would be entering into advance training to become a catholic priest. Boy, I was shocked and my uncle was completely overcome with joy. I looked at him and I could see tears flowing from his eyes. Eva was crying like a newborn baby. I could not help from crying. Kevin was born a criminal and alcoholic. I believed it was AA and my uncle and aunt's love that helped turn his life around. He was a good example for the whole family as to how a person can change his life if given a little help and lots of love," said Lola.

"If I get out of this mess, I will promise God I will change my life. How do you think my chances are after hearing the family story?" asked Lola.

"Well, young lady, your legal team is the best and I think your chances are very good. We are going to put in a plea of not-guilty by mental disease and mental defect. Your trial will start in thirty days. Remember, I am now the assistant to the lead attorney. The lead attorney is an old friend of your father. He was informed about the situation and has agreed to represent you. He has said that you should have a chance for a new beginning. He believes that your family history has set you up for a life in crime. He will be flying in within a few days. He has a lot of work to do and will need you and your uncle's help," said Ted.

"Let's take a break and go out for dinner?" asked Ted.

"Okay, if you don't mind eating with a colored girl. Give me a few minutes to take a shower and change my clothes," said Lola.

'Ted might be the man of my dreams. It took me all these years and all the things that I have done to find him. I wonder if he feels the same way about me. If I get out of this mess, I will devote my life to living clean. I would like to find my parents and pray that they are okay,' thought Lola as she took a hot shower.

"I am in love with Lola," said Ted to himself. 'She deserves a second chance for happiness. I have loved her from the first time I set eyes on her in that jail cell. She was gorgeous then and she is more gorgeous now. I feel like Redd when he first set eyes on Nina. I understand Redd's feelings that evening. I would like to state the same words to Lola that Redd said to Nina. That is: I want to marry you someday,' thought Ted.

As Ted was looking around the room, he saw a picture of Nina and Redd on their wedding day. He was surprised to see that Lola looked just like Nina. Both were beautiful and at that moment, Ted knew that fate had brought the two of them together. After the trial, he decided that he would ask Lola to marry him.

"I am ready," said Lola.

"Let's drive to New Orleans and have some real fun. On the way, you can tell me how you ended up in a holding cell in jail," said Ted.

"Remember Leroy? The gang leader that I caught selling dope at the club and I had my bouncer put him out? He turned me in for a lesser charge of manslaughter. Leroy killed a man and before he went to court, he wanted to plea down to a lesser

155

charge. Leroy said he killed the man in self-defense. The prosecutor said 'no.' Leroy told him that he could give him some information about an organization called Redd's Club that was doing illegal business in all areas, selling and dealing with kids and underage college students. Therefore, the prosecutor went for the deal. It was a Saturday night and the club was jammed. All the gambling tables were full. The liquor was flowing and the music was going strong. The Gentlemen's Basement had a waiting list. In walked ten police officers and shut us down and asked for me by name. I did not want any extra trouble, so I came forward. I had just come out of the shower and had to put on some clothes. My hair was a mess but at that point, I did not care. I just did not want anyone to get hurt," said Lola.

"They had an arrest warrant and they read me my rights. Sitting on the floor of the cell, I began to wonder how I developed this lifestyle of being a criminal. Then it came to me that I was born into a family of criminals and it was in my genes. Then you walked in and I took one look at you and I knew I was going to have a second chance at a new life like Kevin," said Lola.

That night in New Orleans, Lola and Ted had dinner and went dancing at a jazz club. It got late and they decided to spend the night. As they were booking a room at the hotel, Ted said, "One room with a king-size bed and we are Ted Burch and Lola Burch."

That night, they made love and Lola was finally happy even if it was going to be for a short time. She now had the love of a man who loved her and not for the color of her skin.

The next day after breakfast, they drove back home, and Lola and Ted were ready to finalize Lola's criminal defense.

Within a short period of time while arriving home, Nick pulled up and a second car followed him.

"This is Mr. Robert Wright. He will be the lead attorney on your case. He understands the situation. He was the state district attorney for Louisiana for many years. He has the experience and the knowledge and has influence to win your case," said Nick.

"Your criminal defense is: not-guilty because of mental disease and mental defect. This was caused by growing up in a family that used criminal activity as a way to make a living. That environment caused you to become a criminal. As a young child, you were an alcoholic and once an alcoholic, always an alcoholic. You attended AA for juveniles. You had multiples relapses and had to return to AA. We have the documentation from AA.

"You and your brother made and sold moonshine in high school and college. As a young child, you developed an organizational system that helped to run the organization from day to day. Leroy, who is a witness for the prosecutor, will help us. He will be asked to describe how well-organized the Redd gang was functioning. Without knowing it, he will help win our case. The jurors will fall in love with this beautiful young girl who was abused and raised in such a deep-rooted criminal family," said Mr. Wright.

"Next, I will need to make a list of the entire living family members who were involved in criminal activities. They will be on the witness list," said Mr. Wright.

"I have a few smoking guns. Most defense lawyers normally only have one but we have several. We need to locate your mother and father. I have their social security numbers. I will have them run to see if they have worked or filed taxes. We should be able to locate them that way. If not, we will go

157

to your mother's aunt in Alabama and interview her to see if she can help us. We will find them. They owe it to you to return in response to your criminal defense," said Mr. Wright.

"I have the Harrison family's information – Redd's notes, Nina's diary, financial records, list of all murders, list all names of law enforcement officers that were on the payroll. We also have Zola's family's financial records and history which was compiled by the FBI," said Nick.

"We will ask for total immunity for everyone in your family. With total immunity, no one can come back and file civil lawsuit against the family. In return, we will give them information necessary so they are able to solve old cases, including murder. I believe they will go for it. After all, this is your first offense. You would get off with a light sentence if convicted," said Mr. Wright.

"Let's make a list of what we have. Tomorrow you can present it to the prosecutor," said Nick.

"We won't tell what we have. We will tell him what we can do for him. After he agrees to full immunity in writing, we will give him the list of family members that will need full immunity, and then we will turn over our papers. We will make copies of all papers," said Mr. Wright.

"I have a recording from Lola about the family's criminal activity. That will also verify the papers," said Ted.

"How did Lola know the family history?" asked Mr. Wright.

"My brother and I found our grandparents' papers in my uncle's basement. As for the businesses we ran, we copied them from the information that we attained by reading those papers. My uncle never knew that we found those papers," said Lola.

"I am going to ask if the total immunity applies to anyone who testifies on your behalf. The information that we can give them goes back many years and will solve many cold cases. The law enforcement will look very good in the public's eye," said Mr. Wright.

"When do we go to court?" asked Lola.

"Since I am the new lead attorney, we have been given additional time. Court will start in three weeks. That will give us time to send out subpoenas and get the immunity issues confirmed in writing," said Mr. Wright.

"We will also need to send what we have along with our witness list to the district attorney's office. They in return will send us their evidence," said Mr. Wright.

"Nick, what I will need is the address of my list of witnesses which will include your brother and his wife, and your nephew. Johnny Jones (employee of Off Campus Café), Henry Bryant (employee of Off Campus Café), Eva Harris (Lola's aunt), and Bruce Carson (the longtime friend of the family) will all be on the list," said Ted.

"I need all the witnesses to be here next week so that we can go over their testimony. I do not want any surprises," said Mr. Wright.

"Get the subpoenas and I will have the address ready in a few days. They will show up or go to jail. This is my niece's life at stake and this is their small contribution in helping to give her a fresh beginning," said Nick.

"Mr. Wright, are you anyhow related to Candee and Frank Wright?" asked Lola.

"Yes, they were my parents. I was raised in California, and after their death, I learned that they were criminals. As young adults, they were criminal partners with your grandparents. Most of what I know came from your two uncles and information that was left or found in their belongings after they died. I moved to France and got married. I agreed to return and help you because it was the only right thing to do. My parents got a second chance and now I want you also to have a second chance. I feel like family, so from now on, I want to be called Bobby."

"Are we going to have any trouble with the district attorney's office? Every time I see him, he looks like he is ready to say something but doesn't know how," said Nick.

"I have gotten that feeling too. He keeps looking at me as if he has seen a ghost from the past," said Lola.

"Maybe he has, maybe his past is catching up with him. Time will tell," said Bobby.

Lola did not go back to live at the Off Campus Café. Ted offered to let her stay at his place. She just wanted time away from all that life and have a chance to search for what she wanted. Lola went to visit her great aunt who was her grandmother's baby sister in Alabama. She did not tell her she was coming. She had not seen her for over fifteen years. Aunt Lulu had moved away from New Orleans as a young bride when she married a local preacher.

Alabama was much different than New Orleans; most of the area was still country. After asking questions and getting directions, Lola finally arrived at her aunt's home. The house was a big white classic farmhouse with a large church down the road. The farm had horses, cows, goats, pigs, chickens, and a beautiful golden retriever. As she stepped out of my car, the golden retriever greeted her.

"Hello glorious, what is your name?" asked Lola to the dog.

Lola knocked on the front door and no one answered. She saw that there was mail in the mailbox. To make sure she was at the right place, she looked at the address on the mail. It said Lulu Brown.

Thinking to herself, she said, 'That's right. That's my aunt.'

On the door was a plaque that said: 'Sunshine, Laughter, and Friends are always Welcome.' This made Lola feel good and wanted. As she sat on the porch with the good dog by her chair, she fell asleep.

Lola was dreaming about her life with her mother. Her mother loved to sing, dance, play the piano, and cook. 'God had given her many gifts and she enjoyed using them. Having black blood in her was never a liability for Mom. In fact, she believed it was an asset. Her gifts were inherited from her grandmother who was a black woman and loved life. How my grandmother became a criminal is puzzling to me. It must have been learned,' dreamed Lola as she slept.

"Wake up, young lady. I hope you have enjoyed your nap. Do I know you?" asked Aunt Lulu.

"Yes, I am Lola Harrison. My mother is Zola," she said.

"You look just like Nina. It is as if she was reincarnated. It is so wonderful to see you after all these years. I see you have already met Brandon. He is a very good judge of character. Therefore, you have passed his test. Why are you here?" asked Aunt Lulu.

"It is a long story, but I needed time to sort out my life. I have many criminal charges against me. I will be going to court in a few weeks. I was hoping being out here in God's country for a few days might help," said Lola.

"Your mother is living here. She is a different person than you knew when you were twelve years old. She has changed her life. She does not drink, do drugs, or smoke. She is a member of my church and the music director. The community loves her. She used her money to build a new church for the people of this neighborhood. She started a food bank and shelter for the poor. She works everyday trying to improve the lives of others. With God's help, she is doing a good job," said Aunt Lulu.

"She goes to church!" replied Lola.

"Not only does she go to church but she has been taking piano and organ lessons and plays the music every Sunday," said Aunt Lulu.

"Where is she now?" asked Lola.

"Working, working at the church and food bank," replied Aunt Lulu.

"She will be coming home shortly," said Aunt Lulu.

At that moment, a car putted up and it was Zola. She was still beautiful. With her was a young boy. He looked like Kevin. Zola walked in and was greeted by her aunt in the foyer.

"Lola is here. I have told her about your new life but it is your responsibility to explain to her about your leaving and reason for leaving. Derik will also need to be explained. Tell her the truth and let her decide what your relationship will be in the future. As you know she is in trouble with the law. She knows that you have been subpoena to testify on her behalf. This is your chance to make up for years of lost love of your family," said Aunt Lulu.

As Zola walked into the living room, Lola ran over to her and started hugging her mother. "Mom, Mom, I love you and have missed you," said Lola.

Tears were flowing down from both of their eyes. It was so wonderful that Aunt Lulu was also crying. Derik looked up and asked, "Who is this lady?"

"This is your sister. Her name is Lola," said Zola.

Good smells were coming from the kitchen. "Let's eat and afterwards we can talk," said Aunt Lulu.

The table was being set when Uncle Bert, who was Aunt Lulu's husband, was coming through the door. He was surprised to see Lola all grown up and looking just as beautiful as her mother.

"Well, let's eat and if I can help you ladies in any way, please ask for my help," said Uncle Bert.

Sitting in the living room, Zola started speaking. "My life was a mess. It was a mess from the time I was born. My parents lived a criminal life. I was raised by criminals. That is all I ever knew. I left that life but not my children or husband. I needed my family to be set free from a life of crime. Derik is your brother. I was pregnant with him when I left New Orleans. He had been one of the joys of my life. I pray that you and Kevin will accept him. He needs your love. He does not know of my past. One day, he can be told," said Zola.

"I knew that we would be together one day, but I did not know it would be because of my problems. My lawyer feels that I have a good chance of being found not guilty. My family history of criminal activity is my defense. 'Criminal defense' are the words that my lawyer is counting on that will set me free," said Lola.

"How is your brother?" asked Zola.

"You will be very proud of him. He entered the seminary. He is planning on becoming a priest. He had a bumpy beginning but with Uncle Nick's love and help, Kevin has turned his life around. He will be in court with Dad and other family members to testify on my behalf. You do know that everyone who testifies for the defense will be given total immunity. You will only be asked about the family and me as a child growing up," said Lola.

After a few days Uncle Bert, Aunt Lulu, Lola, and Derik all backed their things to go to Louisiana for Lola's big day in court. They arrived early as requested by Mr. Wright.

Nick and Eva were glad to see the whole gang. This was the first time the family was going to be together. This had never happened before. Lola's problems with the law created a family for the first time. Kevin was going to arrive in two days and Nate would be arriving early in the morning.

Lulu was a good swimmer and could not wait to get into the pool. "I have not been in a pool in many years. I can swim. As a young girl, we went swimming every day at twelve, noon, in the county pool located in the county park. The Red Cross gave lesson every summer," said Lulu.

Before you knew it, everyone was in the pool having fun and acting as if it was going to be the last time they would be together. The cook made a meal that was southern-style and they eat outside in the beautiful yard with a colorful, perfect garden.

Kevin was concerned about his returning to Louisiana, so he paid a visit to his bishop.

"In a few days, I will have to make a journey which will lead me back home where the devil was with me for many years. I need to have the ability to rise above and fight off the devil so that I can help my twin sister. She has been lost for many years but after this criminal complaint is resolved, I believe she will take a different path. After all, we have a common bond that I plan to use to help guide her to God. Bishop, I need your prayers to help me in my duty by God."

"I will pray with you but God will be your guide. This is God's plan for you. Making you an ambassador for God was His plan the day you were born. As an ambassador, you will win in and out of court. For you, it was like crawling into church on your knees like an alcoholic who had fallen into that bottomless pit of hell. God saved you for this day. He stood at the opening of the pit and refused to let you fall. Now you are with Him," said the bishop.

Mr. Wright was up early in the morning of his meeting with the Harrison family. He knew he had to face this family and associates of criminals and develop a defense that the jurors could relate and understand.

"Good morning, my name is Robert Wright. I am the lead attorney and Ted Johnson is my assistant. With your help, our criminal defense is going to win Lola a not-guilty decision. I understand her defense and believe in her. She had no control over the ancestral history of criminals that was her family. I would first like to tell you that everyone that testifies on her behalf has been giving total immunity. This means that you cannot be charged for anything that is discovered in court through your testimony.

"Do not add anything about yourself that might connect you to any murders. Murder is not part of the immunity agreement. Answer the questions; do not add anything. I have documentation that will help the law to solve several cold cases for your immunity. I will call your name from the list.

Nick Harrison (uncle)
Zola Harrison (mother)
Nate Harrison (father)
Kevin Harrison (brother)
Eva Harrison (aunt)
Spook Jackson (partner)
Johnny Jones (employee)
Bruce Carson (employee)
Lulu Dupree (aunt)
Bert Dupree (uncle)

I also have a doctor to testify.

"Everyone here?" asked Bobby.

"No," said Nick. "Nate is not here. He is expected to be coming. I am sure he will be here for court."

"Is there any questions?" asked Bobby.

"If not, this is the order. I want you to enter the courtroom. I believe the prosecutor has something up his sleeve. Therefore, I want to set the tone for this case. Nate and Zola, walk in together. Next, Nick and Eva. Kevin, Spook, Johnny, and Bruce will walk in by themselves. Lulu and Bert will walk in last together," said Bobby.

"Go home and get a good night's sleep and have Father Kevin Harrison to pray for our success tomorrow and that maybe all your lives might change for the better," said Ted.

Ted looked over at Zola and said, "I feel you could use a friend. I have something I found out and I need to tell you and Bobby. Let's go over to my home and have a bite to eat and I will tell the both of you. It might be good or it might be bad."

Ted ordered Chinese food and as they were eating, he said, "I hired an investigator to check into the prosecutor's background. I did this because he appeared to have more knowledge about the Harrison family, more than what was in the discovery reports. Yesterday, I received a report on the good prosecutor. It appears that is from Harrisonville, NC. He is the same age as Redd. The investigator asked around town and found out that his father was the sheriff during the time Mr. Harrison, Redd's father, arrived in the area from Ireland. In fact, the sheriff was the one who led the charge to chance the name of the town to Harrisonville after Redd's father died. The sheriff became good friends with Redd, or he could be called his partner in crime. He was on Redd's payroll. His name is in the ledger that Bobby's father, Frank the accountant, kept. Now you can see how important this information can be. How it can be used, I do not know right now," said Ted.

The next day, Nate was not at the courthouse. Zola entered first by herself. Next, the rest of the group followed. They all sat together like one big happy family. The prosecutor kept looking as each one entered the courtroom. He did not know what Bobby and Ted had found out about him. In fact, he could have been on the witness list to tell the story about this family of criminals. His father was one of them.

The judge entered the courtroom and everyone was ordered to rise. Within a few minutes after sitting down, Nate walked in. The prosecutor's face turned red. He knew he was going to lose this case. Nate knew the prosecutor because he lived in Harrisonville longer than Nick. His father, the sheriff, was the person who told the boys to burn down his father's home after he was murdered by Rita.

"I will now hear the opening statements. Mr. Wright, you are first," said the judge.

"Excuse me, judge, but can we have a side bar?" asked the prosecutor.

"The defense has elected to not have any jurors and to let you decide whether Lola is guilty or not. Can we go into your chambers for a short conference, judge?" asked the prosecutor.

"After reviewing all the discovery information and the background of the witnesses, I have decided that the information supports Lola Harrison's claim of mental defect and decease as her criminal defense is true. I would like for her to seek therapy for her mental problems as part of the settlement. Also, she is not allowed to take part in any form of illegal activities," said the prosecutor.

"Call Miss Harrison in and see if she agrees, and if so, all charges will be dropped," said the judge.

Lola entered the judge's chambers slowly with her head bowed slightly. She knew this could be the end of her life. But for a brief moment, a small ray of hope passed before her. As she looked into the judge's eyes, she knew that God was on her side.

"Miss Harrison, all charges will be dropped if you agree to the following:

Seek therapy for your illness and never surround yourself or get involved

with any criminal activity," said the judge.

"Yes, I agree. Thank you, judge," said Lola.

"Don't thank me. Thank the prosecutor. This is his last case. Tomorrow he is retiring. I believe he will be moving back to a small town called Harrisonville in N.C.," said the judge.

Lola's eyes opened wide and just as she was about to say something, Ted put his hand on her shoulder and led her out of the judge's chambers.

The judge came out and announced that all charges were dropped and the court was adjourned. Everyone stood up and clapped. As Lola walked out with Ted by her side, friends, relatives, and spectators all lined up as Lola walked down the hall and congratulated her on her victory.

Lola looked at Ted and knew that this man was her savior. He had saved her from a life of shame and hopelessness. He was the man of her dreams. She felt just liked Nina when she saw Redd for the first time.

'Was this history repeating itself? My life is still a mess. I first must get my life together before I hope to invite Ted to share it with me,' thought Lola.

Nate and Kevin were staying at the same hotel but the rest of the family was at Nick's home. Nick said, "I want the family to have dinner at my place tonight. I have something to share with you."

Zola walked over to Nate and looked straight into his eye and said, "You are still good-looking and I still love you. I understand that you could never love me again after all that I put you through."

"You did put me through many years of misery, but my love for you has never died. You are more beautiful today than the day I first laid eyes on you. I have missed you and still love you. You are still my wife. If you will have me, I'd like to come home," said Nate.

Tears were flowing down Zola's eyes and she almost fainted when she heard the words 'I still love you.'

"Nate, I have someone you need to meet. His name is Derik and he is your son. He is the baby I was carrying when I left Louisiana. Whatever you did to yourself, it did not work. God has given us a chance to start over. Derik was sick as a baby and needed a blood transfusion. His blood type did not match mine. Therefore, I called the man that I thought was his father and his was not a match either. I called your doctor and he sent your blood type to Derik's doctor and it was a match. In fact, he told me you were the father. You and Derik have a very rare blood type. He looks just like you," said Zola.

"Where is he now? I want to meet my miracle son from God," said Nate.

"You will meet him tonight at dinner," said Zola.

"It is nice to have all the family here for dinner. Nina would have loved this moment. In remembrance of the relatives before us, will our priest, Kevin, say the prayer?" asked Nick.

"Our Father in heaven, this family has taken a long route around the house of God. We are blessed by your forgiveness of all our sins. This meal represents all that is good. Keep us from evil and guide through the light, that we will find peace in our belief in you. Amen."

"That was wonderful. What I would like is for the family to tell a little bit about them because it has been many years since we have sat at a table for a meal," said Nick.

"I will go first," responded Aunt Lulu. "I am the matriarch of the family. I am seventy-six years old and the youngest of fifteen children. As you can see I am black. My sister who was your great-grandmother married a Frenchman in France. They only had one child and, from that marriage, one granddaughter who is Zola. Even though some of you look white, we are black. We have been proud of our mixed heritage.

"I have always been in the church and can't remember not going to church. I married Bert at a young age and he became a minister. We never had any children but we have been blessed with a wonderful church, good family, and good friends. Thank you, Lord," said Lulu.

"I'd like to say something," said Ted. "I am not related but would love to be part of this remarkable family. Lola has told me the family story based on the information she read in her grandfather's and grandmother's papers. After all, you did survive. Not only did you survive, but you also have become honest and caring," said Ted.

Nate was ready to take his turn. "I have been a criminal most of my life. After Zola and I parted, I found God. I used my money to open up a group home for seniors in West Virginia. These seniors do not have much but my staff and I take good care of them. I love my new profession and Zola has agreed to go back to West Virginia and work with me. We both feel good about each other and only want the very best for our children and family. Taking care of seniors is our calling and we will devote the rest of our life doing just that," said Nate.

Turning to Lola, Ted said, "Lola, in plain words, will you marry me?"

"Yes," said Lola.

Everyone clapped and was happy for the two of them. This was truly the high point of the family dinner.

"Okay. Okay, now it is my turn," said Zola. I am black and proud of it. I married a white man and he loves me. I have had some rough times but was blessed by God to be here for the good times. I am serving God now and not myself. I will serve him until my spirit passes up to God. I love my family," said Zola.

"I am a priest but was once lost in sin. The devil had me but God won the battle. God will always win the battle. I was the worst of all sinners. I have destroyed many lives. I pray that God has saved them," said Father Kevin.

"I'm next," said Eva. "I married into this family. I was an FBI agent investigating Zola's parents. I fell in love with Nick and we are having a wonderful life together. That is all I need to say."

"After I speak, I want to tell the family my news. I have always loved the lord. I realized at an early age that crime was not for me. I did not have stomach for that lifestyle. It was in the genes, for I had to fight like an alcoholic every day to keep from following that road of crime. I understood what my niece and nephew were going through. Therefore, I loved them and told them so. I was devoted to them. Today will be a new chapter in Lola's life. My plan for her will develop all her gifts that have been given to her. She is the one who brought all of us together. May God be with her always!" said Nick.

Nick got up and pulled a white sheet off his replica of his dream palace. "This is Harrison Paradise Club. Lola put her home up for sale and I purchased it. I got all the required licenses which included a liquor license. As you can see, it has a pool regulation size with cabanas all around, a bath house, eating areas, bar area, and fifty hotel rooms with tennis courts and a golf course, which is what Redd and Buddy always dreamed about. I am giving it to Lola. She and Ted will be the owners. It will be their wedding present. Tomorrow is the grand opening of Harrison Paradise Club. I have hired all the staff and we are fully booked for the hotel. The penthouse is for Ted and Lola. The guests will start arriving at 11:00 a.m. The guests include local lawmakers who are paying their own way. No freebies are going to be given out at this club. Everyone pays their way. Congratulations on being the new owners of the Harrison Paradise Club!" said Uncle Nick.

"Thanks, Uncle Nick," said Lola. "Thank you for sticking by me for all these years. You have always been positive in your approach to getting my brother and me through those difficult teenage years. We were blessed to have an uncle like you on our side," said Lola.

Everyone got up early to go to the club. Lola said she could not sleep because she was so excited. They had all planned to eat breakfast at the club together.

Harrison Paradise Club was located on thirty acres with a large lake for boating and fishing. As you approached the club, it looked like paradise, with large columns as you entered the main building. The lobby of the hotel was fantastic. A huge glass chandelier hung from ceiling and a winding staircase took you upstairs to the dining room or you could take the elevator. All the hotel rooms had kitchenettes with a wet bar for entertaining. On the thirty acres was a golf course with eighteen holes. The golf course was the prettiest in the state.

Lola could not believe this all belonged to her. She just stood there and looked. "This is where I would like to get married. The family is all here. Ted, let's get married this week. I want my family to be here for my wedding. Kevin can perform the service," said Lola.

The club was so beautiful that it did not need much of anything done to it. The family agreed and Kevin also agreed to perform the wedding. A few friends were invited but it was mainly family.

It happened that Saturday and the weather was perfect. The wedding took place down by the lake. Lola looked more beautiful than words could express. Ted was the most handsome man there. Lola had lived a life as a criminal but developed into an honest, loving, and lovely young lady.

As the wedding music played and the bride walked down the carpeted path, everyone was crying. Kevin said, "Continue to cry, for they are not tears of sorry but tears of joy, Amen."